THE VERDE RIVER KID

The Verde River Kid's raids, robberies and other depredations made him a hero of the Indians and Mexicans. But then the U.S. army, whose job it was to maintain order, sent Lieutenant Pat Leary after the Kid. Leary hounded him night and day, and after a gunfight, captured him. But the Kid had allies as well as enemies, and on the way back to the fort, Leary rode straight into another gunfight . . .

JOHN KILGORE

THE VERDE RIVER KID

Complete and Unabridged

LINFORD
Leicester

First published in Great Britain in 1996 by
Robert Hale Limited
London

First Linford Edition
published 1997
by arrangement with
Robert Hale Limited
London

The right of John Kilgore to be identified
as the author of this work has been asserted
by him in accordance with the
Copyright, Designs and Patents Act, 1988

British Library CIP Data

Kilgore, John, *1916*–
    The Verde River Kid.—Large print ed.—
    Linford western library
    1. Western stories
    2. Large type books
    I. Title
    813.5'4 [F]

ISBN 0–7089–5132–5

Published by
F. A. Thorpe (Publishing) Ltd.
Anstey, Leicestershire

Set by Words & Graphics Ltd.
Anstey, Leicestershire
Printed and bound in Great Britain by
T. J. International Ltd., Padstow, Cornwall

This book is printed on acid-free paper

1

An Old and Secretive Land

FROM Tuzigoot to Moctuzuma's Castle, which wasn't a castle nor did any of the Moctuzumas ever see it, it was a crumbling adobe ruin, inhabited by an assortment of tribesmen from Pima to Hopi to Navajo, and Apache was half a day's ride. There was a reason; it had a dug-well of pure, cold water in a territory where any kind of water was rare. Tuzigoot was a sleepy place, nothing more than a village of mud structures where people rarely lingered, while the ruin called Moctuzuma's Castle at least had an air of mysterious antiquity, with good water.

The area was rough, mountainous, spectacular in early spring after the rains, otherwise barren, brown and inhospitable.

The Verde River probably fed inland dug-wells for a fair distance. It came close to both Tuzigoot and Moctuzuma's Castle. Farther south it veered southwest where the Superstition Mountains forced a change of course in the direction of the village called Mesa.

The only people who had devised methods of survival in this country were Indians, half a dozen tribes of them consisting of half a hundred clans. Their *rancherias* were scattered throughout the mountains, valleys and, rarely, in the open grasslands. They had survived as hunters. Some, such as the *pueblo* Indians who had large mud villages and were sedentary, were agriculturists. Others raised livestock, mostly goats but also sheep and cattle.

They accepted the inroads of whites with the identical aloofness as they had accepted those who preceded the whites — Spaniards and later Mexicans.

With some exceptions they were not warlike, as pastoral people rarely are. But there were occasional flare-ups.

These were usually put down by the army whose jurisdiction included all the area which did not have statehood status.

The natives, Indians, Mexicans and 'breeds of every shade and conviction, were united in their dislike of soldiers. It had been that way for several hundred years beginning with Spain's cascqued *conquistadores* followed by Mexicans and most recently the US Army whose power over an enormously vast area of unmapped territory was bequeathed to the United States at the signing of the Treaty of Guadalupe Hidalgo.

The natives of this southerly territory, accustomed to conquerors, upset and as disenfranchised as they were, paid little heed to newcomers. In their daily lives little changed, in their customs and beliefs nothing changed. They did not like soldiers whether their war horses wore the *naja* of the Spaniards, carried the snake and eagle pennant of Mexico, or the US flag, known among them as 'the bloody gridiron'.

They were different from one another in many ways, even their languages, attire, their customs were different, but above all else there was a unity of conviction about men wearing uniforms, and this made it possible for a *gringo* named William Smith otherwise known as the Verde River Kid to elude capture when soldier patrols criss-crossed the land seeking an outlaw who systematically robbed stages, banks, bullion shipments from mines and afterwards simply disappeared behind the facade of expressionless faces, bland stares of indigenous people who, after the army departed, laughed, turned back to their *metates* for grinding *maize*, their other routines of existence and awaited the next arrival of soldiers.

Invariably the army was accompanied by interpreters because, although natives usually understood English, to strangers and soldiers they professed ignorance by using the Mexican term *no habla English*.

It was as a recent commandant at Ford Dix had said many times, while fuming and red in the face, like talking to rocks. But his statement was not altogether correct; there were half-breeds and Mexicans who would, for money, seek information for the army.

For Major Erskine at Fort Dix, these sources at times seemed to deliberately send cavalry in the wrong direction. They might ride fifty miles north and the Verde River Kid would rob a bullion shipment or a stage carrying army payrolls fifty miles southward.

The major, a florid, short-tempered veteran of the Civil War complained to Washington and got back words of encouragement and routine praise for doing a good job. As he once told Lieutenant Patrick Leary, a place built on a swamp several thousand miles away which was inhabited by paper-shufflers and gaggles of people whose sole interest was politics as it might affect their tenure and had not the faintest idea where the Territory of Arizona was, Fort Dix might as well be located on the moon.

The last time the major ranted Patrick Leary had just returned from three weeks of combing the area around an Indian pueblo atop a plateau where it had been reported Indians were hiding the Kid. He had found nothing, was tired and not in the mood for Erskine's outburst but endured it until the major paused for breath, then quietly said, "The next time we're told where he is, north, south, east or west, we might do better to ride in the opposite direction."

The major leaned on his desk staring. "Odds are three to one, Lieutenant, you'll go in the wrong direction."

"Maybe, sir, but maybe not," the junior officer said. "On the ride back I did some calculating. Let's say the next informant says the Kid's going to raid a bank up north. We accumulate information beforehand on who is expecting a gold shipment or where there's a bank that's recently received money. Or maybe where some wagoners are carrying a load of gold down into Mexico."

Major Erskine arose, paced to the stove, turned and said, "It's still big odds."

The lieutenant arose, he was a lean, tall man with grey eyes and a bronzed complexion. He was in his early thirties but already had grey at the temples. "We cut the odds, Major. We send a patrol wherever an informant says the Kid will strike. We also send patrols to the other likely places."

"Lieutenant, it'd damn near strip the garrison."

Pat Leary considered the older, heavier man. "Yes sir, it will come close, but if we don't outguess this son of a bitch no one's going to get promoted — or transferred to a more civilized post, are they?"

This remark would strike home as Pat Leary knew it would. The major hated the Territory, Fort Dix, the natives, even the unpredictable weather. He returned to his desk, sat down, clasped both hands and scowled at the opposite door. His final words were delivered in a growl. "Work it out, Pat."

Leary returned to the parade ground. It was late springtime, the waves of heat which would arrive shortly were beginning to tint the sky a faded, brassy blue.

He went to the stable area, found Sergeant Mulvaney sweating rivulets even without his tunic as he doctored a large bay horse for a bad gash in the right shoulder.

Henry Mulvaney was bullnecked, sorrel-haired, pale-eyed and built like a bull. His face bore scars from having been tested many times. He turned when the lieutenant walked down the runway, mopped off sweat and fixed his small blue eyes on the officer. "What did he say?" Mulvaney asked.

Leary sat on a bench, pushed out his booted feet and regarded the sergeant. They'd had a special relationship for three years. It had taken half that long for the relationship to mature because Henry Mulvaney, an old campaigner, just naturally disliked officers.

"He said for me to work it out." Leary made a crooked grin. "He was worried about stripping the fort of men."

Mulvaney sat down, again mopped sweat off and said, "Strip it? Who'n hell is he afraid of? No one's tried to fight the fort since Hector was a pup."

The lieutenant yawned, unbuttoned his tunic half way and let go a ragged sigh. "What do you think about sending Sandy out to poke around?"

Mulvaney leaned against the wall as he replied. "I expect it can't hurt. For a fact whoever buys him the first drink will give him information, an' it won't be no good. It never is."

The officer nodded agreement. "But we got to start somewhere." He arose. "The mail's due tomorrow. Old Windy knows everyone's business. With luck he might even be carrying a box, it's close to payday. You want to talk to him?"

Mulvaney nodded and also arose. "Better a sergeant than a lieutenant."

"You got something that'll oil his pipes?"

Mulvaney nodded without answering. It was against regulations for enlisted men to have whiskey on the post.

Lieutenant Leary went to the hutment he had shared with another officer until his hutment-mate had been transferred. He dug into his 'possible bag', for the bottle, mixed the contents with lukewarm water, kicked off his boots, loosened the rest of the buttons of his tunic, tossed his hat at a wall hook and missed, lay back on the bunk, took two long swallows, stoppered the bottle, pushed it under the mattress and slept like the dead until the evening bugle sounded.

It was one of those lingering, soft dusks that made the land appear less hostile, made the heavens reflect eternal promise, as he headed for the mess hall.

The major did not appear for an excellent reason, he too had had a drink or two and slept through the bugle call, which did not really matter because his second-in-command had conveniently waited until everyone was seated before the order to eat.

The following morning Lieutenant Leary went to the hutment of Sandy Gomez, the half-Mex scout. He went early in order to make the visit before Sandy started taking his 'medicine'.

The scout was a dark man with black eyes and hair — with a touch of grey at the temples. He was possibly in his fifties, it was impossible to be accurate guessing someone like Gomez's age. He was a raffish, untidy individual and welcomed the lieutenant to his hut, built against the north-east wall of the palisade, with a broad smile. The visit was brief, the lieutenant needed the best information Gomez could get about the Verde River Kid. Gomez promised to ride among the settlements and would leave this day.

Gomez had a squaw at a place called Dune, which was not secret, but by orders, scouts, civilians in army service were not allowed to bring families inside to live with them. It seemed on the surface to be an inhumane order but it wasn't. Three years earlier a small child ran out to greet a returning patrol, ran among the horses and got his skull crushed by one kick.

Lieutenant Leary went to the command post where the major was presenting his orderly-clerk several handwritten letters to be recopied. He nodded at Leary and jerked his head.

In his private cubicle the major stood behind his desk as he said, "The son of a bitch did it again."

Leary nodded. It was not wise to ask questions particularly of someone with the major's irascible disposition.

Erskine sat down and gestured for the lieutenant to do the same. "He's a thorn in my flesh, Pat. He didn't stop the wagon. This time he rode into the mine about midnight, rousted out the head man, made him open the safe and made off with three-four thousand in raw gold."

"Where?" Leary asked.

"The Clover Leaf Mine above Tuzigoot day before yesterday. He gave the superintendent a note for the army. I got it right here. In'ian brought the news late last night. The note says 'Catch me if you can, you red-faced old bastard. I know everything you do. Verde River Kid'."

Erskine raised a red face. "Red-faced old bastard! Pat, I want him brought here alive. I'll red-faced-old-bastard him until he can't stand up without help."

There were two other lieutenants at the fort, one named Bulow and one named Hardesty. Pat Leary knew what was coming and thought he'd sidestep it when he said, "Bulow's a good man, Major."

Erskine nodded brusquely. "Yes,

indeed, but neither him nor Hardesty knows the country as well as you . . . I know, you just came off a long scout . . . " Erskine did not finish the sentence, he paused to fish in a drawer for two cigars, one of which he offered Pat Leary, who accepted it and leaned toward the lucifer. When they were both comfortable the major continued where he had left off. "But you got some idea of the Kid's routine an' his territory." The major squinted through fragrant smoke, waiting.

It was a long wait. Leary tipped ash then said, "He won't be anywhere near that mine," and paused to trickle smoke thoughtfully. "So that eliminates the Tuzigoot area. Major, I sent Sandy out this morning."

Erskine snorted. "He believes every lie they tell him. Pat, what we need is an In'ian workin' for us."

Leary faintly smiled. "Not likely, Major."

"For good pay, found, an' a hut inside the fort?"

14

"They aren't too interested in money, they get their found from their own livestock or by hunting, an' I've yet to meet one who'd even come inside the fort for a band of horses an' a Winchester rifle."

The major leaned back trickling smoke and gazing at the younger officer. "Pat, don't tell me what won't work, tell me what will!"

"I gave you my idea yesterday, Major. But it can't be worked out until we get good information from reliable natives. When we get that the rest should be simple; have three patrols out." Leary considered the tip of his stogie. "We don't know that it'll work, but we damned well know what won't, don't we?"

Major Erskine expectorated toward the brass cuspidor with unerring accuracy. He plugged the cigar back into his mouth and spoke around it. "All right. Like I told you yesterday — do it. I'll send someone to Tuzigoot to soothe ruffled feathers an' get all the

15

information he can get." The major stood up, the sign a meeting was terminated. He had one more thing to say before Pat Leary headed for the door.

"That bastard's been runnin' loose for two years. If we get an Inspector General out here, you know what kind of a report he'll write back in Washington? I don't want to die a major any more'n you want to die a lieutenant."

With one hand on the latchstring Lieutenant Leary nodded and said, "It'll take time but I'll hustle things along. Major, if we succeed — catch him — the amount of time it took to do it won't seem too long."

Outside the sun was climbing, the corporal who was stable-master waited until the lieutenant was passing then spoke. "Gomez rode out hour or so back."

Leary nodded about that and would have continued on his way but the corporal had one other thing to say.

"Last night an In'ian come to the gates with a note for the major."

Leary knew this too and nodded again.

"He bedded down in the hay. When I come in this morning his horse was still eatin' but the tomahawk was not around. He come in half-hour ago, smiled, rode out, and what was he doin' for the couple of hours he didn't come for his horse? Want me to guess — spyin'. They're slippery'n a greased pig."

Leary went to his hutment. He had no idea how long it would take for the information to be available which would enable him to put his plan in motion, but he knew Major Erskine, a blunt man with a short fuse.

A burly figure filled his doorway, waiting to be invited inside. It was Sergeant Mulvaney. He swung a chair, straddled it and retold the story of the Indian to which the lieutenant said, "You want to go after him?"

"Someone sure as hell should — sir."

Leary nodded. If the Kid had given the note to the mine superintendent and he had given it to the Indian to deliver, it was possible — just barely — but possible that the Indian would be able to provide the information about details of the robbery, and, with any luck, the robber.

"Take a squad," Leary said and watched the bull-built, carroty-haired man walk briskly in the direction of a barracks.

It was a long shot, the note-bearing Indian might know nothing, but at least he lived in the Tuzigoot area and something Pat Leary had suspected for a long time was that the Verde River Kid was some kind of two-bit hero among the natives. For a fact they never saw him, did not know him, and had no idea where his hideouts were. They said all this with faces as blank as stone.

The major's idea hiring a native as a scout had nothing wrong with it. It just would not work out for a simple reason; the natives had an inbred dislike of uniforms of whatever kind.

Over the generations they'd had reason to mistrust and dislike soldiers.

2

A Plan

WILLIAM SMITH — the Verde River Kid — had tight curly brown hair and somewhat coarse features. He was slightly less than average height, had a muscular build and a smile that reached from ear to ear.

He had a winsome personality and one attribute which separated him from most outlaws and renegades, he was not cruel. He was also, so the legend said, deadly fast and accurate with either his belt-gun or his saddle-gun, but that may not have been true; it was, however, essential to the more than life-sized myth about him.

He bought horses where most outlaws stole them, and he enhanced his legend by liberally spreading money, or in some cases raw gold, around.

He was a reincarnated purely south-western Robin Hood. It was said among lawmen he deliberately projected generosity and principles in order to be sure people would hide him, but the fact was that the Verde River Kid was an outgoing, generous — and mighty clever individual by nature.

One of the stories claimed he had broken the leg of a massive blacksmith who was beating hell out of a small wizened and harmless old drunk, with one shot from a distance of 200 feet.

Stories of his exploits were almost as numerous as his actual deeds, which was interesting because he had only been active in the Territory for two years, maybe a tad longer.

Wanted dodgers described him fairly accurately, but without a picture identification was difficult; half the men in the Territory, excluding the very dark ones, were medium height with brown eyes and an average build.

What contributed to his elusiveness

was that he invariably knew when and where to strike. Pat Leary had a notion about that; the money he gave out with a generous hand had assured him informants throughout the areas where he raided, which was probably true except for the tribesmen. Money meant less to them than ideals, and the Verde River Kid personified a solitary individual who could and did successfully defy authority. The Indians in particular needed a legendary figure who could do that. As for the Mexicans, they had always needed a hero who would make any kind of authority look ridiculous.

How he had raided that mine near Tuzigoot was an example of the Kid's capability. Presumably the only people who knew there were bags of raw gold, ready for shipment in the superintendent's office, would be men who worked at the mine, not a Mexican nor an Indian among them.

Clearly, he had waited until all but the patrolling guards were asleep, and just as clearly he had known which house the superintendent lived in. What else he knew was anyone's guess, but when the superintendent was awakened by something cold and hard in his ear, nothing mattered except taking the Kid to the safe and handing him the little leather pouches. He had not done what was common practice, he had not knocked the superintendent unconscious with his pistol barrel, he had tied him to a chair with his mouth taped closed.

The Mexicans were by nature addicted to unrealistic explanations. They said the Verde River Kid was a *fantasma* returned to this world to rob the rich and succour the poor. If that were so there was the handwritten note to Major Erskine. Few superstitious people believed ghosts used pencils to write notes.

He seemed to prefer dusk or later for stopping wagons and stages but it was known that he had robbed thriving mercantile establishments as

23

well as banks in broad daylight.

Inevitably, someone tried to prove the Verde River Kid was not one outlaw but two. Their reasoning was that two holdups the same day at places eight or ten miles apart, could not be accomplished by one man, but any horseman worth his salt knew better. A good mount could cover the distance without more than pausing to catch his second wind.

Fourteen days after the Tuzigoot mine raid, the Kid stopped a stage coming south from Williams. It was accompanied by two rifle-bearing outriders. He had forced it to stop for boulders in the road and had patiently waited until an argument between the whip and the gun guards about who would remove the rocks ended in a compromise before he came up behind the rock-carriers.

That coach, so it was said anyway, had been carrying six thousand spanking-new dollars from the Denver Mint to be delivered to a place near Mesa called McHenry where the brick bank was waiting for its first shipment of new money.

Of course Major Eskine heard of the robbery, this time by an irate, whining bank official and later went to express impatience with Lieutenant Leary whose reply was that he had been gathering scraps of information which did not appease the major and when the lieutenant mentioned that some of his information had come from Sandy Gomez the major threw up his arms and stamped back across the parade ground, slammed the door of his office and glared at his surprised clerk who had been reading a telegram. In fact he had the telegram in hand when the major charged in, went to his office, groped in a low drawer for his bottle and was raising it when the orderly knocked once then entered. For seconds the enlisted man looked at the bottle in Erskine's grip, then cleared his throat, stepped forward and placed the yellow paper on the desk.

Major Erskine used one hand to raise

the paper, kept his other hand with the bottle in it below the desk top. The clerk waited for the explosion to come. He was an old campaigner with two years to go before retirement. His customary expression was no expression at all.

Erskine looked up with colour rising. "Two weeks," he snarled. "The son of a bitch will arrive in two weeks."

"Yes sir. That's what it says."

"I know the gawddamn thing says! Someone from the Inspector General's office will arrive within two weeks. Why?"

"I don't know, sir."

"No warning. Somethin' got them upset. Hell, every letter I've received since bein' here had been a commendation. Now this!"

"I'd like to make a suggestion," the enlisted man said with exactly the right degree of deference an old campaigner knew to use. "Sure as hell when he gets here he'll hear about the Kid. Maybe they've already heard in Washington."

"I know that, damn it!"

"Sir, if Mister Leary could speed up his plan an' maybe catch — "

Erskine sprang up still clutching the bottle. "Go tell him I want to see him at once!"

After the enlisted man's departure Major Erskine put the bottle in its drawer without opening it, sat down and glared at the far door. Anyone from the Inspector General's office was trouble four ways from the middle.

When the lieutenant walked in the orderly discreetly closed the door after him. Major Erskine did not say a word. He handed the yellow paper to the lieutenant, clasped his hands and was silent until Pat Leary put the paper back on the desk, then the major said, "Two weeks, Pat. If there's been complaints about that damned outlaw sent to Washington, you got two weeks to find him, skin him alive and hang the hide out to dry."

Lieutenant Leary gazed dispassionately at the major until the red-faced senior officer said, "Well!"

"I'm not quite ready," Leary said.

That caused the explosion. "You're ready, bucko! By Gawd you're ready! You got until tomorrow to start the manhunt. No! I don't want to hear a word. Dismissed, Lieutenant!"

When Leary passed through the orderly did not look up from a sheaf of papers he was studying. Not until the outer door closed, then he gently wagged his head.

Pat Leary hunted up Lieutenants Bulow and Hardesty, explained what he wanted them to do, and why, told them to have their troops ready after mess in the morning, and went down to the stable looking for Mulvaney, who was in the wash-house doing laundry.

When the lieutenant walked in Mulvaney was wringing cloth until the muscles in his neck were rigid. He tossed the wrung-out shirt in a basket and waited.

Leary explained about the telegram, the major's agitation and that he and Sergeant Mulvaney would take C Troop due west, with Hardesty and Bulow taking troops A and B in north-east and south-westerly directions.

Mulvaney said," You get any reliable information about where the bastard might raid?"

The lieutenant wagged his head. "Nothing reliable, so I'm left with no choice but to make a guess."

"An' maybe ride in the wrong direction," said the sergeant.

"Maybe. The major's orders are to get in the saddle."

"Did you tell him you wasn't ready?"

The lieutenant looked steadily at the sergeant without speaking. Mulvaney sighed. He understood. No one argued with commanding officers.

Leary had a question. "Did you find that In'ian who brought the Kid's note?"

"No sir, an' we tracked him all the way to Dune. After that every barefoot horse track looked like dozens of others. But I visited with Sandy last night. He's got a woman at Dune."

Leary nodded slightly. That was no secret.

"He said his woman told him one of her clansmen was in Dune day or so ago, an' told her the tomahawks knew where the Kid figured to raid. Over at Harcuvar."

Leary frowned. "There's nothin' over there, Henry, just some In'ian *jacals* an' mountains."

"A pack train headin' for Messico, Sandy told me."

"When?"

"His woman said it'd reach Harcuvar settlement in about three, four days."

"A pack train goin' to Mexico? The Kid don't bother with trade goods."

Mulvaney agreed. "He don't, but since we'll be patrolling westerly . . . "

Leary nodded. On his way to his hutment it occurred to him that Sandy Gomez's woman might have deliberately relayed this information because she believed it, and had been told the tale to make the army react

30

as it had in the past by riding in the wrong direction.

He hunted up Bulow and Hardesty, told them what Mulvaney had said and warned them to keep scouts out and to be alert, things it was not necessary to say and after he left the other officers agreed that Leary was worried, which he was. Not entirely because the westerly ride might end up making him look foolish because he had been duped, but because he was beginning to develop a genuine antipathy toward the Verde River Kid.

The major came to Leary's hutment, sat down and said, "Remember, I want him alive."

The lieutenant gazed at his superior. Arthur Erskine had been through the war, he had been a professional soldier all his mature years. He had to know that capturing someone who was sure to resist was impossible if there was shooting.

Erskine saw the look he was getting and hunched forward in the chair. "If

31

it can't be done, all right, but I want this one more than I've ever wanted one taken alive."

Leary quietly said, "I'll do my best, Major."

Erskine arose, slapped Leary lightly on the shoulder on his way to the door, paused briefly to say, "But no promises, eh?"

"Major, I don't even know that I'll be riding in the right direction."

After the major had left Pat Leary dug out his bottle, poured in some warm water from a canteen, tipped in whiskey and went out front with his tin cup to sit on the bench beneath the frond-shaded *ramada*.

It might have been, as some swore was the truth, that Sandy Gomez could smell whiskey at 200 yards, but true or not the scout appeared, stared at the tin cup in the lieutenant's hand and said, "Summer is coming, no?"

Leary almost smiled as he held out the cup he had barely touched and said, "It always does, don't it? Sit down, Sandy. Mulvaney told me what a woman at the Dune settlement said about the Verde River Kid goin' to attack a pack train."

After swallowing twice the scout jerked his hand up and down very emphatically. "He was her cousin. I asked if he lied. She said she'd known him since they were little kids and he never lied."

"Sandy, her cousin came to Dune to tell her the story. Maybe he don't lie, but just as likely he told her something he had heard, which don't make it believable. You understand what I'm sayin'?"

Sandy had half-drained the cup. He relaxed on the bench with his back to the wall and his feet shoved full out. His breath would have brought tears to the eyes of a brass monkey.

"*Teniente*, I have those same thoughts. I wondered, but you know how people are. Maybe they lie to throw the army off, an' maybe they got some reason to want the Kid killed. *Quien sabe?*

Who knows? But I believe the woman an' she believed her kinsman, so where does that leave us?"

Leary did not reply for a long time. There were many people, mostly respectable storekeepers, stagers, bankers and Gawd knew how many others who would not shed a single tear if the Verde River Kid rode into an ambush.

The scout interrupted Lieutenant Leary's reverie. "The last stage he robbed was coming south from Williams, no?"

"Yes."

"It was stopped half-way along."

"Yes."

"That was north of Mesa, north of McHenry a fair distance."

Leary said, "If you're gettin' at where he might raid next that could be east or west."

"*Seguro!*"

Leary looked at the empty tin cup. "You want a refill?"

"Yes, *jefe — gracias!*"

They went inside, Leary made the mixture stronger this time and the scout, sweating rivulets, sank into a chair broadly smiling. "Before you came here, before the major came here, even before roads were made between settlements it was customary to use pack trains and mules for everything."

Lieutenant Leary watched the scout sweating and becoming more mellow by the moment. "That was long ago," he said.

Gomez continued to smile. "*Colonel* — "

"Lieutenant not colonel an' you're drunk, Sandy."

As though there had been no interruption the scout went on speaking. "Do you know what *verde* means?"

"No."

"It means green. Did you know in the old days gold was always sent by mule train through the green mountains of springtime."

"No, I didn't know that."

Gomez's black eye went to the lieutenant's face and stayed there. He was still wearing that wide smile when he said, "That mine in the Tuzigoot country he raided — I heard it had pouches of gold ready to be taken away."

"What of it?"

"*Teniente*, suppose they would, or some other *miens* would decide the roads were too dangerous an' maybe use the old pack-train trails."

Gomez's wet-black eyes did not move. Lieutenant Leary said, "Didn't those old-time pack outfits go north, not south?"

"Yes, but *teniente*, the old trails go south almost to Mesa then took an easterly trail through the mountains until they could veer northward where there was better travelling country." Gomez put the empty tin cup aside and straightened up in his chair. "*Teniente*, suppose the Indian told my woman about the pack train going to Messico because he really thought it was goin' there? But nowadays there is something else."

"What else?"

"*Teniente*, south of Harcuvar through the mountains there is the railroad. They use the pack train through the mountains because no one will see it. Indians. They wouldn't care. You see? The pack train could be loaded with raw gold from a mine, it would be hidden for most of the way south by mountains. It could meet a train some miles north of the Gila River. *Comprende?*"

Lieutenant Leary sat looking at the scout for a long time before arising to lead the way outside, back to the bench where, as they sat down he finally spoke. "Sandy, I'll ask the major if you can go with us."

"But you know the country, Lieutenant."

"Not as well as you do, an' we might need an interpreter."

Gomez gazed across the sun-blasted parade ground. "It will be a long ride through rough country. Very dry country."

Leary considered and came up with the right answer. "I'll bring along some medicine. Now, I'll go settle it with the major."

Sandy watched the lean, weathered figure making long strides in the direction of the command hutment, spat at a passing lizard, missed, shoved up to his feet, squared his shoulders and started walking. He concentrated on the front of his hut which kept him from veering from side to side, breathed deeply and sweated.

Those who saw him cross the grinder were not fooled. Gomez's deliberate measured stride, erect posture and raised head could have been mistaken by strangers as the movement of a sober man but there were no strangers; the watchers watched and winked at one another.

The major was drinking coffee as black as original sin when Pat Leary walked in. He offered the lieutenant a cup which Leary declined and requested permission to take Sandy

Gomez on his sortie to which the major agreed without hesitation. But he had a question. "How're you going to keep him whiskeyed-up — take a pack horse?"

Leary smiled at the intended joke, did not say how he planned to provide the medicine Gomez needed and returned to the yard.

Alone in his hutment he had second thoughts; suppose it was really a pack train of animals laden with trade goods for Mexico? If that turned out to be the truth, the Verde River Kid would not only have the last laugh but would certainly spread the story of incompetent soldiers.

Gomez had been drunk, but not too drunk. What he had said could only have been recounted by someone who had known this country since childhood and who, for a fact, was as sly as a coyote to figure a reason for a pack train to be passing through mountainous country where pack trains had not passed in ten or fifteen years.

Leary alternately worried and schemed. He and his riders would have to be as *coyote* as Apaches. They would have to travel through mountainous country where Indians had secret *rancherias*, and they would have to do something the army had never been either noted for or good at; they would have to be both silent and invisible.

3

The Trail

THE invisible part was not difficult; after two days they spent the entire third day in camp and rode at night.

Being silent was something else. Barefoot horses made no noise in rocky territory but shod horses did. There was a way to mitigate that, common among renegades and raiding broncos, cover the hooves with sacking or canvas.

The army provided no such equipment nor did it appear to be essential until the night of the fourth day when Sandy inadvertently led them close to a hidden spring, with no idea — which he should have had — that there was a small *rancheria* at the spring. He should have known because he had known about the spring, and he certainly knew as scarce as good water was, anywhere a free-flowing source of it existed there would be people as well as animals, particularly dogs.

Sandy came out of his reverie with the first sound of dogs and reined southward where there was no trail. It was close to dawn before he halted in the bottom of a gorge to say there was no other source of water for another six or eight miles toward the hill Harcuvar country, and it would be too far, too long a ride before daylight.

There were fifteen men — sixteen counting the scout — and as the lieutenant said, the horses would require water before the following evening. Sergeant Mulvaney as well as the other enlisted men made a dry camp without once speaking to Sandy Gomez, and by noon of the following day their barely restrained annoyance was heightened as the sun stood directly overhead. An arroyo was not the most comfortable place to be during an Arizona summer day.

The men had canteens, the horses stood in weak shade and sweated. Lieutenant Leary recognized the hint of trouble before Sergeant Mulvaney came into the puny shade where the lieutenant was sitting and said, "There's grumblin'. The men don't like bein' in the bottom of this canyon without water for the horses."

Leary's answer was curt. "I don't like it either. Maybe come sundown we can find water."

Mulvaney shook his head. "Not before we reach the old way station. That's what Sandy says."

Leary considered the bull-necked, non-commissioned officer. "It's Gomez, isn't it?"

Mulvaney nodded.

"Henry, one day's not goin' to be the end of the world."

The sergeant said something that brought the lieutenant straight up where he was standing. We're sittin' ducks in

43

this canyon an' Hoskins went out with Kendall an' saw In'ians along the west rims watchin' us. Lieutenant . . . "

"How long ago?"

"Maybe quarter of an hour ago."

"Pick the best men. Climb out of here from the south. Catch at least one of 'em."

Mulvaney looked almost pained. "Lieutenant, can't none of us climb out of this canyon without them In'ians see us doin' it."

Pat Leary arose and dusted himself off. "Go over to the horses and mingle. I'll try to climb up there but I need a diversion."

Mulvaney's scowl melted. "They'll see you climbin' up there."

"Maybe not if you make enough of a diversion."

Mulvaney watched as the lieutenant buckled his belt with the holstered pistol. As Leary was turning toward the first thornpin thicket Mulvaney said, "I'll strangle Gomez for leadin' us down in here like pigeons in a shootin' gallery."

Leary made a humourless smile. "That ought to create a diversion." He ducked among the flourishing undergrowth where he was lost to sight in moments.

It was hot, hotter in the arroyo than outside of it. The air did not move, none of the little errant breezes that were common during late spring and early summer arrived.

Climbing toward the west rim of the arroyo would not have been particularly difficult for someone not crouching from one stand of undergrowth to the next. For the lieutenant it was time-consuming and unpleasant. He could tolerate the last of the annoyances because, for twelve years the army had consistently provided him with discomfort of one kind or another, but the passage of time troubled him, and it was no comfort knowing that Indians spying on soldiers rarely did this hastily.

By the time he was close to the rim

the sun had moved, which provided shade in the canyon but not up where the lieutenant lay lizard-like scanning in all directions.

He hadn't heard shouts from the bivouac nor had he taken the time to stop climbing to look below, but evidently Mulvaney had indeed created a diversion because a short, dark Indian appeared on horseback.

He did not go to the rim but made a mourning-dove call to attract the attention of other broncos. One appeared not far ahead as though he had come out of the ground. He and the mounted Indian conversed before the mounted man turned back the way he had come.

Leary watched where the Indian on foot disappeared in underbrush and began belly-crawling slowly.

When he thought he was close enough he palmed his handgun, eased underbrush aside and peeked ahead.

It wasn't one Indian, it was four of them. One, with greying braids wearing an army-issue campaign hat and who had a polka-dot short apron suspended from his belt in front, was profiled to the officer.

The lieutenant eased his pistol forward an inch at a time. One of the Indians was facing in his direction but like the others was concentrating on the buck with greying braids, who spoke calmly using a minimum of hand gestures. That bronco and his companions gave the lieutenant an impression of something like simple curiosity. They were definitely not hostiles. There remained isolated bands of hostiles, mostly in the deeper recesses of the mountains but in general the Indians were reconciled to a countryside under the domination of overwhelming numbers of whiteskins.

Leary let the pistol-barrel sag as he spoke quietly. And although his voice was unexpected none of the broncos evinced anything more than mild surprise.

The man with braids said, "Come

out. We saw you start up here."

Leary arose, holstered his belt-gun, moved around his protective bush and stopped. The Indians eyed him stoically. The braided one gestured as he said," Sit down."

Leary sat.

The braided man had a question. "Why are you skulking? There are no hostiles here."

The lieutenant also had a question. "Where is your *rancheria*?"

The Indian raised an arm toward the west. "Across the narrow place, maybe a mile from the old way station." He lowered the arm. "We used to live at the way station. There's been no one there for many years, but two weeks ago some men came an' moved in, so we moved out. We used to live along the Hassayampa River but it got too crowded."

"How many people in your *rancheria*?" Leary asked and the Indian shrugged like a Mexican before replying. "Thirty, counting very young ones. Why? Is the army going to round us up and drive us to a reservation?"

The lieutenant eyed the other Indians. Only the man with braids and one other bronco were not cross-breeds. He hung fire before replying to the braided man. "No. The army's not interested in your band."

"But you are here."

"We are here to wait for a pack train."

The older man solemnly nodded. "To out-ride for it. Well, there has been no pack train through Harcuvar country since I was young."

Leary considered the older full-blood. "What is your name?"

"I have two names. One is Yellow Dog Man. The other is Charley Runner. You want to know how I got that name? Because years ago I outran on foot two cavalry horses with men on them. What is your name?"

"Patrick Leary."

"Captain?"

"Lieutenant."

"Do you want us to help out-ride the pack train?"

"No. I want you to go back to your rancheria, tell no one you saw us, and don't leave your camp no matter what."

The older man's dark eyes with muddy whites widened. Pat Leary awaited the next question but evidently the Indian decided not to ask it. He arose. "When will the pack train come along?"

Leary could not give a definite answer so he said, "Soon. I am not sure." He held out his hand. As they shook he said, "Don't let anyone from your camp go find the pack train an' tell its drovers there are soldiers waiting."

Again the older man's eyes widened and again as he released the lieutenant's hand, he said nothing, simply turned and spoke in his own language so that when he strode in the direction where horses were tethered, the other Indians followed him.

Lieutenant Leary skidded back down

where his troopers were waiting, told Mulvaney what had been said on the rim and gave the order for saddling up.

This time when Sandy Gomez took the lead his orders were to find water, and because the only water he knew of in the area was over the crest of the mountains and down the other side, he took that route. If it worried him that the sunlight reflected off so many brass accoutrements it did not show. The lieutenant had said lead the company to water and that was exactly what he intended to do.

There had once been a way station midway between the Harcuvar Mountains and, going southward, the Santa Maria River. Also southward there was a healthy creek but it lay in open country; the original builders of the way station had preferred less exposed country. In their day Apaches routinely combed the entire countryside. The adobe way station with mud walls three feet thick and a sod roof impervious to fire arrows, had successfully withstood a number of attacks. What hostiles couldn't do the railroads did. They had sidings along their lines where they stopped to take aboard everything from horses and mules to bullion boxes and their protectors.

Indians in the Territory never successfully stopped railroad trains. They tried by racing alongside and firing both arrows and bullets, but no horse on earth could stay abreast of a moving train for more than a hundred yards or so.

There were a number of abandoned and dilapidated way stations. They were more common where wheeled traffic could pass, but there remained some whose access was old overgrown pack-train trails.

The way station Sandy Gomez led the patrol to had withstood the passing of time fairly well. Its builders had extended pole rafters two feet beyond the walls. Adobe, which withstood time and heat, had to be protected from rain, which washed adobe into mounds of mud.

The corrals out back had not aged very well, some of the posts were rotten and some of the peeled log stringers were missing. It was not difficult to guess what had happened to them. Indian fire rings of stone kept fires from spreading during the cooking of meals and dry wood was the best kind because it gave off no detectable smoke.

The dug-well had a pulley but no rope. There was a leaky bucket which, until it had swelled leaked more water than could be brought to the surface. It was sweaty, back-aching work to haul up water for the horses, whose thirst seemed everlasting.

Lieutenant Leary sent Sandy and the sergeant to locate the *rancheria*. His idea was to have a couple of men intercept any Indians going north.

They made a camp without fire, to which the troopers were accustomed, and when daylight passed the customary sentries were posted.

When Mulvaney returned in darkness to report neither he nor Gomez had seen Indians leave their camp. The lieutenant fished in his saddlebags for a bottle, unscrewed the cap and passed the bottle to his sergeant and, although Sandy hadn't been around, he appeared soundlessly, grinning like a Cheshire cat.

Leary handed him the bottle. Gomez swallowed three times, afterwards blew out a flammable breath, wiped his mouth with a soiled cuff and said, "There is a hill up the trail about a mile."

Leary nodded, considered giving Gomez the bottle, decided against it because he needed an alert, wide-awake scout, and watched Gomez pass from sight outside in darkness.

There was no moon. Mulvaney went among the troopers who were sufficiently relieved to be out of the canyon to pass jokes and relax.

One trooper, possibly about Mulvaney's

age, said, "You can't trust tomahawks. They'll sneak upcountry an' tell them *arrieros* soldiers is down here waitin'."

The sergeant was as aware of this as anyone. He sent the old campaigner and two other men to go watch the *rancheria*. The old campaigner looked disgusted with himself as he led off in darkness.

A soldier named Topper waited until the others were beyond earshot before remarking about tired men sleeping instead of watching.

Mulvaney had faith in the campaigner but not much of it in his younger companions. He was satisfied the older man would make certain the younger ones wouldn't fail in their duty.

The old way station could accommodate all the men who wanted to sleep under a roof, which did not include those who had bedded down in ancient mud buildings before and had awakened with flea bites.

The following morning Sandy returned to report no sign of a pack train or the dust it would stir to life. That night the lieutenant sent Mulvaney. When he returned in the morning it was with the same story. No pack train in sight and no dust.

Lieutenant Leary began to have misgivings. If those tomahawks had gone north to pass word of a soldier patrol waiting at the old way station, as sure as Gawd had made green grass the pack train men would veer either eastward or westward. If they did this they would have rough going. Breaking trail was bad enough but in mountainous country with laden animals it would be slow, arduous work. Worse, if an outlaw was watching he would also change course.

He decided the following morning before Mulvaney returned to send men in both directions, told them to find high places and watch for movement and dust, and at the same time to avoid being seen.

When Mulvaney returned, listened to what the lieutenant had said about sending men to watch easterly and westerly, the sergeant dryly said, "Well; there's dust a fair distance on the trail north. I hope, if they got outriders they don't see the men you sent away."

Leary was standing near a broken table. He pulled the thing around and perched on it. The table had one leg gone — no doubt as kindling for an Indian fire — but it held together as he regarded the sergeant.

Mulvaney hadn't shaved in days, his uniform was rumpled with prominent sweat stains. He had too much carroty-hair for his cap to cover. He seemed unaware of his appearance as he eyed the lieutenant.

"Might be a good idea to send after them men and bring 'em back, Lieutenant."

The officer nodded and asked a question. "Could you make out whether it was a pack train?"

Mulvaney hid the annoyance that question aroused in him but his reply was laced with sarcasm. "I couldn't make that out, but there's considerable dust — and who in the hell would be comin' south on this trail?"

Lieutenant Leary grinned. "Take my spy glass, see if it's them."

"Yes sir. An' them lads you sent out?"

"I'll send someone to fetch them back."

After the noncommissioned officer had departed Lieutenant Leary went among the men. The horse-water detail was hauling up the bucket and cursing about having to draw the bucket which one horse could empty without a pause.

Lieutenant Leary rode to the *rancheria* where he had been seen approaching and the grey-braided Indian called Charley Runner was out front of a shelter that resembled an inverted beehive. It had blankets across its domed roof. There was a smoke hole from which was rising more burning-wood fragrance than smoke.

The lieutenant dismounted, shook his head at the youngster who came to hold his horse and with his left rein on one hand he asked Charley Runner if anyone had left his camp. The older man wagged his head. "Only some boys who had to see about their rabbit snares . . . Tell me something, Lieutenant — "

Leary interrupted. "Charley, those *arrieros* must not know there are soldiers waiting for them."

The old man's dark eyes with muddy whites widened. "You don't figure to outride for them. I didn't think so. Why would soldiers outride for a pack train goin' down to Messico?"

"It's not the pack train, Charley."

The older man slowly smiled. "I wondered. Something didn't figure right. But you won't tell me."

"Did you ever hear of an outlaw named the Verde River Kid?"

"Of course I've heard of him. Everyone has . . . is that it? Why would he come here?"

"Maybe he won't," the lieutenant said. "Maybe the pack train is carryin' trade goods down to Messico."

"But you don't think so."

"I don't know what it's carryin' but the Verde River Kid has robbed so many bullion wagons among other things — it's someone's idea the pack train might be carryin' raw gold."

"To Messico, Captain?"

"Lieutenant . . . No, down as far — maybe — as one of those railroad sidings between the Gila River an' Hohokam."

Charley Runner looked around. People were watching him and the uniformed stranger. He looked back and said, "I think you need help. Is it true the Verde River Kid comes at dusk or in the night? If it is he will see some of you or smell your smoke. Captain, I have some good scouts. They can become part of the dirt, the brush. I don't think he will come riding down the trail in plain sight, will he? I can have scouts watch him long before he gets down here. I think you need our help."

Pat Leary glanced around at the

motionless, still Indians. He thought they were about evenly divided between full-bloods and half-breeds.

Charley Runner spoke again. His speech was always measured, deliberate and slow. He said, "This one is like a snake. He can disappear while you are looking for him. Like a *fantasma* . . . maybe he is one. You go back, keep your men quiet, no fires. Wait. We can find him if he comes into our country."

"If you find him," the lieutenant said, "don't try to capture him."

"No. That's your job. They tell me he can shoot out the eye of a lizard from a long ways. You go back, Captain. I'll visit you maybe tomorrow."

"Lieutenant, not captain."

Charley Runner smiled enigmatically and walked away.

4

Mixed Signals

HENRY MULVANEY had not been born a sceptic but after so many years of soldiering he had become one. After listening to what the lieutenant had to say about his visit with the braided bronco, Mulvaney eyed the officer closely before saying, "What you done is give an old In'ian the initiative. Major Erskine would turn purple."

Leary's reply was offered with a slight smile. "I trust him, Henry."

"He's an In'ian, Pat, an' right now we don't need no double-crossin' tomahawk. Suppose I take Sandy an' hide near the camp an' see what ol' braids will do?"

Leary's reply was dry. "Whites never been good at sneakin' up on In'ians, Henry."

"Haven't they now? That's the biggest myth of 'em all. We been successfully sneakin' up on In'ians since we come to this country."

The lieutenant shrugged. "You'll know if they catch a whiff of you. If they do, come on back."

Before departing the sergeant said, "Someone ought to take the spy glass an' watch that dust."

Leary had already made that decision. He nodded, waited until Mulvaney was gone then went among the troopers, selected the old campaigner, handed him the telescoping spy glass and sent him on his way.

Heat came, men sought shade, sweated, drank water and either dozed or held desultory conversations. When the lieutenant appeared among them they accepted his presence without making changes in whatever they were doing or saying.

In mid-afternoon Sandy returned to say the broncos were going about their customary chores, none had left the camp, and before Sandy had returned the bronco with braids had appeared in front of their place of concealment amid some rocks carrying a full canteen.

Lieutenant Leary grinned.

Sandy ignored that. "I told Mulvaney the old screwt more'n likely knew we was out there when we first arrived."

"What did he say?" Pat Leary asked.

"Not a word. He put the canteen on a rock and walked back the way he come."

"Mulvaney stayed?"

Sandy nodded. "There never was a more pig-headed Irishman than him. He stayed, drank from the canteen and when I told him it was no use he said for me to go back if I wanted to but he figured to let them In'ians know he was watchin' 'em."

Lieutenant Leary said, "That's pure Mulvaney."

Gomez was not quite finished. "For lack of somethin' to do me'n Mulvaney counted In'ians, but they'd pop into them huts, three more would pop out so we give up ant counted horses. Counted 'em three times. Mulvaney said some were gone. He said he knew that from also countin' the pad saddles outside the huts. Maybe six or eight was gone."

Sandy licked parched lips. The lieutenant rummaged for his bottle and handed it over. Gomez pulled on it like an orphan calf on a new teat before handing it back. Within moments he brightened and departed.

For Lieutenant Leary the question was not about missing Indians but where they had gone and if they were as seasoned at being invisible as Charley Runner had implied.

Meanwhile he awaited the return of the old campaigner. It was not a long wait, but the day was moving along. As the trooper handed back the spy glass he reported that by his count there were eight pack animals — not horses but mules accompanied by what seemed to be an unnecessarily large number of *arrieros* and outriders.

The lieutenant asked directions to the top-out and left with the spyglass. He did not return until close to dusk and was welcomed by a breeze coming from the north, filling the area between mountains with an invigorating freshness.

Mulvaney was sitting in the shade of a massive mud wall and arose at sight of the lieutenant. He followed Leary inside, sank down on a three-legged stool, a miraculous survivor of the previous Indian residents, accepted the bottle Leary offered, handed it back and said, "That old screwt sent kids to my hiding place. I couldn't understand them an' they couldn't understand me, but I knew what old braids was doing — making me look ridiculous — so I come back. His camp was shy some bucks, an' bein' a bettin' man I'd lay ten to one they went to find the pack train an' tell 'em we're waiting down here."

The lieutenant tucked the bottle away as he said, "I don't think so. I was on that knoll for more'n an hour watchin' the pack outfit. It's got gun-guards ahead, behind an' on both sides, but it's comin' along the trail like no one's worried. It'll be here early in the morning."

Mulvaney gave up trying to get comfortable on the stool and stood up. "What do you want to do, go meet 'em or let 'em come here?"

"Let 'em come here. They're not our objective."

"Lieutenant, the Verde River Kid is no fool. By now he's got to know we're here. Most likely them tomahawks told him."

"Henry, there are too many outriders with that train for it to be carryin' trade goods."

"Then that'll be too many for the Kid to try to hold up."

"Maybe. I don't think us being here or those gun-guards will stop him, unless he's lost some of the guts he's supposed to have. He can raid while they're here or after they leave here."

Mulvaney looked incredulous. "With their gun-guards an' us behind them?"

"Don't seem likely, does it?" the officer agreed. "But he rode a hell of a distance to get in our area an' all those armed outriders mean there's somethin' valuable in the packs, which he probably knows more about than we do. Henry, he's got to do it, or at least try to do it."

Mulvaney went to stand in the doorway as he dourly said, "That's crazy."

Pat Leary would have agreed but the sergeant departed. Leary reconsidered, got the bottle, swallowed twice and tucked it away. As the day advanced heat which had been kept at bay throughout the day began to infiltrate the old building, but it did not get hot, just uncomfortably warm.

After nightfall a sentry called a challenge that alerted everyone. When Charley Runner rode in, troopers with guns stood like statues.

He swung off, dropped his reins and

asked for the lieutenant. A trooper looking mildly hostile took him inside and left him.

Charley entered the candle-lighted small room where Pat Leary was waiting. The lieutenant motioned toward a chair but Charley Runner squatted. He smiled slightly in the poor light. "I watched you on the little hill. Someday I will get one of those glasses that make things come close. I have seen them before."

Pat Leary sat in a chair. "You sent men out," he said.

Yes. They went north on both sides of the trail and watched. Those mules carry heavy loads. But they aren't Mexican mules."

Leary nodded. The army bought big Missouri mules. So did most muleteers who needed large, strong animals.

"There are many riders with guns. I don't think they are carrying trade goods, do you?"

Pat Leary smiled. "No, I don't." When that was all he said the Indian nodded. "All right, but we don't worry about the pack train, do we?"

"No."

"Well, my men scoured the mountains, even the old *anasazi* caves. There was no sign of the Verde River Kid. No sign of any strangers. Maybe he can fly. I heard years ago down in Messico there are men who can fly. Do you believe that?"

Leary did not say whether he believed it or not. He said, "He's out there, Charley — somewhere."

"I think so. I put my best sign-readers to scout for him. Is there a reward on him?"

"More than one, Charley. But remember, your men are not to try to catch him."

"Then we won't get the reward."

The lieutenant considered his reply before offering it. "I'll tell my commanding officer how much you helped."

The Indian straightened up to depart as he said, "Maybe we should capture him," and walked away.

Leary caught him before he left the building. "Charley, just find him. I'll do my damnedest to see you get the bounty. Just find him, don't try to capture him."

The Indian left the building, went to his dozing horse, got astride and rode back out of the bivouac without looking left or right.

In the morning there were clouds with soiled rims, which meant rain; at least the possibility of it.

The horse detail had to take the animals farther out, all the grass and browse close by had been cropped down to dirt.

The watering detail was surly, in fact too much inactivity made most soldiers grumpy. Where Sandy could usually raise a few laughs all he got this morning was hard looks.

Mulvaney said he had alerted the men to the arrival of the pack train, which appeared to break the monotony a little.

Leary went to the northerly knoll with his spy glass. This time he could make out individual faces, even the knots of the two hitches, one a diamond the other a squaw hitch, on the pack animals. One man in particular intrigued him. He rode on the east side of the trail by himself. The other riders did the hazing, this particular man acted as though the over-all responsibility was his.

In Leary's glass he looked older, more weathered and more warily watchful. Twice outriders rode back. He conversed with them each time before they loped ahead to take their places among the gun-guards.

The lieutenant had, over the years, become acquainted with several mine operators. The man he watched was a stranger to him. He wore a belt-gun and had a Winchester in the saddle boot on the near side. He wore his hat tipped forward and occasionally expectorated.

Leary rode back to the way station where the animals had been brought in for watering. The troopers hauling up the bucket as well as the ones actually watering the horses either did not note the officer's passing or deliberately ignored it.

Mulvaney showed up looking fairly presentable except that he hadn't shaved and his hair was still too long. He too had watched the pack train, but without the spy glass. The lieutenant told him what he had been able to make out and Mulvaney mentioned what had been on his mind since dawn.

"The Kid knows we're here, an' by now he's made a study of all them armed outriders."

Pat Leary nodded and leaned against the mud wall waiting for the rest of it. Mulvaney didn't make much of a pause. "He can't raid 'em once they get here. In fact one man alone, even with a Gatling gun, which he don't have, couldn't do more'n get himself killed if he tried to stop the pack train after it leaves here."

Pat Leary eyed Mulvaney without blinking. "So far you haven't said anythin' I don't know."

Stung, the bull-built Irishman said, "He ain't goin' to do it. He's had time to see everythin' an' figure his chances. From what I've heard about the son of a bitch, he's not a fool. That bein' the case, considerin' everythin' else, he's seen everythin' an' my guess is that he's gone back, give it up."

Lieutenant Leary nodded slightly. He'd speculated about this and had arrived at the same conclusion. "An' if you're wrong, Henry, an' he raids the pack train?"

"How? In Gawd's name how can a lone renegade even think he can do it? Even the dumbest one wouldn't try it now."

The lieutenant did not disagree with that either. He simply said, "It's his move, Henry. If he don't try a raid, fine, then we can go home. But if we left now, for instance, an' he tried a raid, the pair of us would be wheelbarrowing horse droppings for the rest of our enlistments."

Mulvaney was prepared to say more when the lieutenant spoke first. "We got to wait until the pack outfit arrives. I'll talk to the head In'ian, warn him. If he don't act worried, we wait until he's on his way then — maybe — head for home. But we waited this long an' another day won't make much difference."

Mulvaney glowered. "Them In'ians . . . "

"What about 'em?"

"More'n likely there ain't a buck among 'em as hasn't raided pack trains. That one with braids. I wouldn't trust him as far as I could throw him. It could turn out the Verde River Kid couldn't begin to raid the pack train the way them In'ians can."

To end this Lieutenant Leary said, "It's possible, Henry. It could happen."

"But you don't think it will?"

"I think their spokesman is too smart

to even think of it while we're in the Territory."

Mulvaney departed with a wrathy stride. Lieutenant Leary blew out a long breath before going to find Sandy to tell him to ride up the trail with his right arm raised, palm forward, and guide the pack train in.

A negroid-looking bronco rode in bareback carrying an old Sharps carbine. The sling had two droopy eagle feathers dangling from it. A sentry stopped him. He leaned, handed the trooper a scrap of paper, whirled and rode away sitting scornfully erect.

The sentry handed Sergeant Mulvaney the paper. He read it, scratched and went looking for the lieutenant.

Leary read the note and gazed at the sergeant, who said, "All right; I never said they can't all be trusted. They found shod-horse sign comin' from the north-west an' ol' braids has two of his best sign readers trackin' the rider. Hell, Pat, it could be a pot-hunter, maybe a lost greenhorn."

Leary pocketed the scrap of paper, smiled without humour at his friend and said, "Go up the trail. Find Sandy and lead them all in."

The back of Mulvaney's neck was red as he walked briskly in the direction of the horses.

No great amount of prescience was required among the watching troopers who had seen Sandy Gomez ride north and who now watched the sergeant go in the same direction. They already knew the pack train was within a few miles of the way station.

Lieutenant Leary went up the easterly sidehill where thorny underbrush was thicker than the hair on a dog's back with his spy glass. He found a tiny clearing where a bedraggled tree grew, got into what little shade it offered and raised the glass.

The pack train was not moving, a crowd of mounted men were out front, so many it was impossible to see Gomez in their midst. When the sergeant appeared the swarm of heavily armed men broke apart enough for Leary to see Sandy. He had a rope round his neck.

When Mulvaney rode up the lieutenant could imagine what he said because the rope was swiftly removed, most of the outriders gave way, except for one man, the dark, weathered individual Leary had noticed before.

He and Mulvaney conversed. Once, the sergeant raised a fist in the direction of the way station. The other man said something aside, his guards and muleteers closed in again and as the weathered man held out his hand, palm up, one of the men behind Mulvaney poked him over the kidneys with a carbine barrel. Mulvaney handed over his belt-gun, turned and started back at a slow walk. Leary almost smiled. Maybe prudence had indicated that Mulvaney surrender his sidearm but Pat Leary knew the sergeant well enough to know he was seething.

He went back to the way station, passed word about the imminent arrival of the pack outfit, did not mention Mulvaney, and told the watering detail to stand by. One of the detail loudly groaned. Another one was bolder, he asked the lieutenant why the men with the pack train couldn't water their own livestock.

Leary said they could, and walked around to the front of the old building in time to see, first, the dust, then a squad of armed men out front looking ahead where soldiers were watching with undisguised interest, and behind them mules one behind the other, more outriders and the *arrieros* whose duty was to care for the mules, they were all Mexicans.

That weathered dark man pushed past his gun-guards. When he was close enough to see the officer he removed his hat and made a gallant little wave with it.

Mulvaney rode past the lieutenant without looking left or right. He was rigid in the saddle and red-faced. To be disarmed by a civilian was something he would never be allowed to forget.

Not just the back and armpits of Gomez's shirt were soggy, the entire garment was soaked with sweat. He rode up to the lieutenant, swung off and in a barely audible voice said, "They thought I was an outlaw. They was goin' to hang me."

Leary did not take his eyes off the dark man as he said, "In my left-hand saddle-bags, an' don't take more'n two swallows."

5

A Night Ride

THE weathered man, whose name was Carter Alvarado, dismounted, handed his reins to a mule-man, removed his right glove and smiled as he introduced himself.

He had tawny-tan eyes, a square jaw, whisker-stubbled face and his attire was pure south-west from the Mexican Chihuahua spurs to stained Stetson hat. He wore his holstered Colt slightly more to the front than was customary. He and the lieutenant went inside. The *arrieros* dumped packs, produced collapsable canvas buckets and smilingly took over the job of drawing water, something the soldier-detail was willing to watch without lifting a hand.

Carter Alvarado was not quite as

dark as his men were and in most ways he acted more *norteamericano* than Mexican, which was understandable. His father had been a *gringo* named Amos Carter, his mother had been a Mexican named Maria Elena Alvarado.

He declined the lieutenant's offer of whiskey, which was a surprise, and offered the lieutenant a little dark Mexican cigar, which Pat Leary accepted and put in a pocket. His one and only experience with Mexican stogies had made a believer out of him.

Alvarado tipped back his hat, studied the soldier for a moment then said, "I didn't know you'd be waiting to help us. As you saw I have fifteen armed outriders along with my pack-train-tenders. Did Mister Hamilton request this soldier escort?"

Pat Leary considered the bottle before answering, decided not to and gazed at the burly, amiable 'breed. "You have heard of the Verde River Kid?" he asked.

Alvarado spread his hands. "Who hasn't?"

"We think he will try to raid your pack train."

Alvarado's tan-tawny eyes sprang wide open. "One man, alone by himself? No. He must have many men."

Pat Leary knew nothing about that, although he had wondered about it. "He rides alone."

Alvarado slapped his leg. "He must be crazy. Do you know he is in the area?"

"Well, all I know is that some In'ians told me. They didn't find any sign of him."

"Then he isn't here, is he?"

"I'd sure like to believe he isn't, but I'm here to make certain he don't try a raid."

Alvarado shook his head in disbelief. "The army sent soldiers to protect a pack train against one man? Lieutenant, I've seen the army do some things that didn't make me think highly of it, but this is the stupidest. No offence; you have your orders. You didn't answer whether Mister Hamilton did this?"

"Who is Mister Hamilton?"

"He's the superintendent of the Lady Luck mine up near Hualapi."

"Was it his idea to send your load by pack train?"

"Yes. We're to meet the railroad at the Gila Bend siding. Lieutenant, this is so unbelievable . . . I understand, you follow orders, but you have a troop of soldiers. I have thirty men including fifteen specially hired outriders. Mister Hamilton does not trust the roads, the Lady Luck has lost several shipments to outlaws. Maybe they are waiting over beside one of the regular roads." Alvarado smiled showing strong white teeth. "It will be a very long wait, eh?"

The lieutenant shoved the bottle back into his saddle-bags, leaned back studying Carter Alvarado. "My sergeant thinks the local In'ians might help the Kid."

"What do you think, Lieutenant?"

"The In'ians scouted you up. Their spokesman don't seem to me to be treacherous."

Alvarado gave an eloquent shrug, he clearly shared the popular view of Indians. "How many Indians, Lieutenant?"

"It's a small *rancheria*, about thirty, forty of 'em counting women and pups."

"How many men? Maybe about ten or fifteen?"

"Likely," the lieutenant assented.

"Well, if they want to try with or without the Verde River Kid there will be squaws wailing and pullin' out their hair."

Mulvaney appeared in the doorway staring straight at Pat Leary, who said, "Something, Henry?"

"Come see, Lieutenant."

Leary nodded without making a move to leave his chair. "Directly, Henry."

Mulvaney remained stubbornly in the

doorway. You better come, Lieutenant."

As Pat Leary arose so did Carter Alvarado whose big Chihuahua spurs rang as he followed the two soldiers out into the dazzling sunlight.

There was a crowd of Alvarado's men mingling with soldiers. A large mule wearing a defiant expression was being held by one of the *arrieros*.

Not a word was said as the officers and the pack-train *jefe* approached. The crowd gave way. There was a pair of heavily reinforced mule packs on the ground. One had most of its leather-edged top torn loose. Alvarado spoke to the man holding the mule in Spanish. The *arriero* answered in the same language. The mule, he said, had stumbled over the packs and had kicked. It was a large, powerful mule, which it had to be to do the damage this one had done.

Lieutenant Leary and Sergeant Mulvaney were standing like statues, not the least interested in the mule or the damage it had done.

Carter Alvarado walked up beside them, looked down and let go a long, uneven breath. Scattered around the torn *alforja* were rocks, some with specks which glistened but these were few, most of the rocks were no larger than fist size, the kind of rocks which were cast aside slag from a mine pit, pure tailings, absolutely worthless.

The old campaigner spat amber, looked at Alvarado and dryly said, "All them pack bags got the same stuff in 'em, mister? If so you're carryin' rocks to a country where they sure-Lord ain't needed."

Alvarado stepped forward, picked up a rock, rolled it in his hand, turned and offered it to the lieutenant, who took it, glanced very briefly at it then tossed it back where it had come from.

Carter Alvarado spoke brusquely in Spanish to the *arrieros* who hastened to the other packs. Alvarado strode slowly and impassively among them. Each *alforja* was loaded with the same kind of rocks.

He went by himself to the front of the way station, sank down on an ancient bench bolted to the wall and stared straight ahead. When the lieutenant came over Alvarado said, "I'd like some of that bottle, if you can spare it."

Leary went inside, got the bottle, returned, sat down and handed the bottle to the man, who took one long pull and handed the bottle back.

He said, "Why did he do that to me?"

"Who?"

"Frank Hamilton."

"Didn't you look in the packs?"

"No. When I rode to the mine the mules were packed and the men were waiting . . . why?"

Lieutenant Leary leaned back and shoved his legs out. "Want me to guess, Mister Alvarado?"

Alvarado did not speak but he nodded his head.

"Because he sent the gold by a different pack train. He needed your outfit with all those men an' guns to look like the real one. I'd guess he knew the word would get around. You got a lot of riders. All it'd take would be for one to tell his wife or sweetheart a pack train was goin' to haul raw gold."

That did not, at the moment, seem to trouble Alvarado as much as the fact that he had been duped, had been made to look like *el papilla*, the Mexican term of derision meaning a fool. What *el papilla* really meant was 'a turkey'.

Mulvaney came over and jerked his head. The lieutenant gave Alvarado a light slap on the shoulder before following the sergeant around the side of the massive old adobe building where Mulvaney said, "Ain't this nice? We been settin' here like frogs on a log. You know what I think? The real pack train is travellin' either east of us in the Harquahala country, which is rugged as hell, or westerly, which is better territory, not so rough an' brushy. I'd guess that outfit will head for the southerly siding."

Lieutenant Leary gazed past his friend where troopers were dumping stone from the *alforjas* with the aid of the gun-guards and the *arrieros*. He said, "Go find Charley Runner, he's got broncos scoutin' out and around. See if they've found sign of another pack outfit. An' Henry, show some respect to the old man. Whether you like him or not he tried to help us ant right now we need help."

Mulvaney walked away with a purposeful stride. Lieutenant Leary returned to the shaded old bench. As he arrived Alvarado was putting the whiskey bottle aside and wiping his lips.

Mulvaney was disgusted. He did not ride fast and once he saw two tomahawks watching him amid some rocks. He did not even look in their direction. He arrived at the *rancheria* with the sun low enough to make him squint.

Lieutenant Leary took Alvarado around where a meal of boiled jerky was being prepared. The *jefe* sat on the ground and ate from a tin plate without meeting any of the glances cast in his direction. Afterwards he returned to the old bench, ignored the bottle and when Pat Leary came up Alvarado said, "The son of a bitch. He wouldn't trust me. You know how many loads of ore I've hauled for him?"

Pat Leary sat down. Shadows were thickening, some of the day-long heat was gone but not all of it. "He did trust you," he told him. "That's why he sent you — to leave a trail. If you hauled for the mine he knew folks would know about it, an' my guess is that he figured you'd be the one to lead the mule train because folks knew he trusted you."

Alvarado said, "You sound like a priest. They always got a reason. For everything; fire, floods, men being used as fools to fool other fools."

Leary did not argue. He did not know a mine operator named Hamilton, had never heard of the man before today. Nor, at the moment, was he especially interested in a man named Hamilton nor even one named Alvarado.

He leaned back and shoved his legs out. *Four to one the real pack train was lightly loaded and travelling fast. There would be no army of gun guards to raise dust.*

He said, "Son of a bitch!"

Alvarado's head came around. "Mister Hamilton?"

"No. The Verde River Kid."

Alvarado relaxed. "How would he know?"

Pat Leary made a wild guess. "Ask someone who works at the Lucky Lady . . . maybe your Mister Hamilton. How much pay dirt was being moved?"

"He didn't say. When I got there everything was packed and ready. All I had to do was lead off. But I can tell you one thing, because I hauled many loads, it would be raw gold."

"Gold is heavy. How many pack animals would you guess there is?"

Again Alvarado had no answer. "I didn't see no other pack animals at the mine compound. I got no idea how many — "

"You didn't see any pack animals?"

"I just told you," Alvarado replied and slowly straightened on the bench as he and the lieutenant gazed at each other with the same thought. Alvarado said, "It went first. It left the compound in the night before I got up there the following morning."

Pat Leary sat in silence for a while then wagged his head. "If it wasn't packin' as much weight as your outfit an' left ten or twelve hours earlier . . . What I'd give my wages for a year to know is how much weight it's carrying an' how many animals are in the train."

Although Alvarado's thoughts had been diverted, he still had anger in his heart for the mine operator who had duped him. "I want to meet the *jefe* of that pack train. Face to face, *mano y mano*."

Pat Leary looked around and spoke irritably. "Forget Hamilton, forget what he did to you. I want to find the Verde River Kid an' as sure as Gawd made persimmons he's going to raid that other pack train. Especially if it's travellin' light with no outriders."

The lieutenant stood up. Alvarado also arose. He considered Leary's expression in the gathering dusk and said, "What are you going to do?"

"I'm going to saddle up the company an' ride all night if I got to. I want to be at that damned siding an if the Kid's not there I'll backtrack him if I got to ride my butt to the quick. Mister Alvarado, I want that son of a bitch!"

The call of a challenging sentry held Pat Leary's attention. Moments later the elderly bronco with grey braids rode up and sat looking at the men on foot, then slid to the ground and, with the left rein in his left hand he squatted, indicating this was going to be a palaver. Leary and Alvarado returned to the bench.

Charley Runner got straight to the point. "My scouts been north and east. One scout, Spider Woman's son, went south. For no reason. I told them to go north and east. Maybe a little to the west. Spider Woman's son never did what he was told. As a little boy he went his own way."

Alvarado leaned forward. Lieutenant Leary put a hand on Alvarado's leg. Interruptions caused the spokesman to ramble.

"Spider Woman's son went south. A pack train passed that way in the night. Four mules, six riders."

Alvarado had a question. "Last night?"

"Yes. I sent Spider Woman's son to track them. If he found them I gave him my soldier-mirror to signal with."

A 'soldier-mirror' was a polished steel mirror used by the army for heliographic signalling.

Alvarado stood up, so did the lieutenant but slowly. He went over and held out his hand. Charley Runner

95

arose, brushed palms with the soldier then said, "We will go after the pack train."

Leary said, "No! Leave that to us. We'll watch for your bronco's sun-signal come morning."

"Then," complained the older man, "we will get none of the reward."

Pat Leary's reply was short. "You will get all the reward. Charley, if the Verde River Kid sees a sun-signal — "

"How will he do that?" the spokesman said. "He will be behind the mule train. He will be signalling back, behind the mule men. If the Verde River Kid is ahead watching the train . . . maybe he has an eye in the back of his head, but I don't think so."

They watched the Indian go to his horse. Before he mounted he looked across the animal's back at the lieutenant. "We can help. No one will see us. We know about this sort of thing."

Pat Leary's reply was emphatic. "No! You've done all you have to do. Now, leave it to the army."

Charley Runner got astride, turned and walked his horse back the way he had come.

Carter Alvarado said, "I'll roust my men," and left the lieutenant standing alone but not for long. He went looking for Sergeant Mulvaney, found him preparing to bed down and told him what Charley Runner had said.

Mulvaney considered his unrolled bed, wagged his head and without a word to the officer went among the troopers telling them they had ten minutes to get their boots on and rig their horses.

The company left in full darkness, silent as the dead, not at all happy about being told to ride but reconciled. This was not the first time and would not be the last time they were inconvenienced. The army was a dispassionate task master.

Horses blowing their noses, the occasional steel horseshoe rattling over stones, men clearing their pipes was the only sound for several miles.

Alvarado had argued like an enraged squaw about being left behind. The lieutenant's statement that this was strictly an army matter left the pack train *jefe* spluttering. His best, most impassioned argument had rolled off the lieutenant like water off a duck's back. He had been left behind, he and his mule-men and his outriders.

Mulvaney rode hunched and dour. Twelve years of this sort of discomfort should have inured him but it hadn't. When the lieutenant gestured for him to ride stirrup the sergeant obeyed but when Leary said, "Another four hours or such a matter to daylight," Mulvaney looked straight ahead without speaking. Lieutenant Leary looked around and did what never failed to elicit a response from the sergeant. He called him by his first name.

"Henry?"

"How're we goin' to find the mule train?"

Leary told him about Spider Woman's

son and his heliograph mirror.

Mulvaney's mood might have been marginally improved but it did not show when he said, "Not until sunrise an' for all we know he'll lose the mirror."

It was a grumpy thing to say and lacked substance but the lieutenant knew his friend. He did not reply. Did not in fact speak again until false dawn arrived with its sickly grey-blue light over the distant horizon. "Henry, keep an eye peeled. He'll signal from west of the trail."

"If he signals!"

By Pat Leary's guess they were no more than eight or ten miles north of the Gila River and the railroad siding was about a half mile north of the river. In some places it paralleled the river no more than a stone's throw away.

Back in the column a youthful trooper, new to the army and the south-west, made a piping call and raised an arm. The flash was brief and not very bright, but it was repeated several times.

Mulvaney's mood changed. He watched the light flash from the westerly slopes, grunted when the reflection came again, several bright flashes from the west and said," Is he behind 'em?"

Leary thought so. "He sure as hell wouldn't signal from in front where they could see the light."

Mulvaney raised his left hand with the reins in it. The country was levelling out, what upthrusts lingered were farther to the west and not as formidable as the identical rises had been farther back.

Lieutenant Leary raised his arm to flag for a lope. He wasn't worried about dust, it would rise but visibility for any distance was unlikely to be seen in the poor light of a new day.

They covered several miles before the lieutenant flagged his troop back to a walk. He sent Sandy to scout ahead and westerly. Mulvaney watched

Gomez lope away and wagged his head but said nothing.

The sun, barely visible above the horizon, increased visibility but did nothing to offset the predawn chill. No one was conscious of the cold, every man watched Sandy cross open country in the direction of some distant low hills which appeared to go arrow straight in the direction of the Gila.

The old campaigner riding behind Mulvaney said, "As nice a target as a man could ask for."

No one commented. Gomez slackened to a steady walk and angled toward some windsmoothed hills which offered no real protection, particularly if anyone was higher up, but it was all there was.

He stopped, stood in his stirrups and flagged with his hat. Mulvaney said, "Does that mean to come over there?"

Gomez's waving became more insistent. Lieutenant Leary veered from the old trail with the troop following.

When they reached the scout Gomez held his arm aloft for silence. No one spoke and they became stationary but nothing could prevent the animals from fidgeting.

Mulvaney was looking up the low hill dead ahead when he said, "You hear 'em, Lieutenant?"

Leary nodded but what he heard could be mustangs or even wild cattle. He sent Mulvaney and Sandy southward to find a place where they could see beyond the low spine of hills. There was no such place. The sergeant and scout returned with Mulvaney wagging his head. He said, "It's over the top or nothin', Lieutenant."

Leary motioned Sandy ahead with the column to follow. Before Gomez reached the top-out he dismounted, left his animal standing and crept to the rim where he could see below. In the middle distance was another scattering of low hills but distant from the open country directly below.

He was motionless as a lizard for

what seemed to Mulvaney to be an inordinate length of time before crawling back down until he rose, mounted and returned to the column. He stopped, looking steadily at the lieutenant. "Four mules, six men an' an In'ian pokin' around at the base of the hill I climbed up to look down."

Not a word was said as the soldiers digested this information. For the lieutenant there were two choices, he did not even consider the first one — ride up the hill and charge the pack train down the other side. He flagged with an upraised arm, turned southward and picked up the gait into a mile-eating slow lope.

Somewhere southward there had to be a passageway and there was, but the hill did not lose height until it had to yield where in prehistoric times the Gila had eroded it. There, the lieutenant stood in his stirrups, saw the twin steel rails reflecting belated sunshine, and also saw the large, graded siding.

6

Night Riding

FOR the lieutenant the best option was to cross over the diminishing slope where he could affect a confrontation, and there was nothing wrong with that strategy except for the Indian who was scouting for the pack train.

He was far enough ahead to be in the area where the hill began to slope away to hear riders on the east side of the hill. He started back to warn the pack-train's drovers when a single gunshot sounded and one pack mule went down like a rock.

The Indian had been hired to scout and for no other reason. He put his horse to the nearest slope and sent it scrambling upwards. Behind him there were two more shots.

Only one mule remained on its feet. Audible to the soldiers on the far side of the hill was a shout, and another shout. The words were indistinguishable.

There was a spate of gunfire, too much of it to suggest sharpshooting. There was also the sound of animals running which was followed by several very distinct gunshots.

Pat Leary called for an advance and led off in a lope southward to the lower slope where the troop could cross without much effort, a reasonable and logical thing to do.

The gunfire dwindled to an occasional shot and when the soldiers crested the hill and plunged down the far side the gunfire stopped altogether.

Three dead pack mules lay almost in a straight line. Several saddle horses were running with reins flying. They ran into the line of soldiers and were captured.

Other saddle animals had been held fast by their riders. One dead *arriero* lay sprawled, the other five men were flat behind dead mules whose laden *alforjas* provided excellent protection.

The five men had fired where a pair of swiftly moving specks were growing smaller by the minute.

One of the *arrieros* sprang to his feet gesturing wildly in the direction of the fleeing rider driving a pack mule ahead of him. This man saw Sandy Gomez and erupted into non-stop Spanish. Of the other men three were Mexicans and two were *gringos*. It was one of the *gringos*, who grounded a long-barrelled rifle and leaned on it as he considered the soldiers. When Pat Leary halted this man called to him. "The son of a bitch got off with the lead mule."

Leary dismounted, growled at the agitated *arriero*, went closer to the *gringo* and asked who had run off with the pack mule.

The *gringo* was a sturdily built man in his forties with both ends of his droopy moustache stained coffee-colour from chewing tobacco. He looked at the lieutenant like he might have looked at a child. "Who was he? Mister, he shot them mules from hidin' an' when he was shootin' there was smoke an' he made a run on the mule and drove it away like the wind. An' just how am I to know who he was?"

Mulvaney had taken a dislike to the *gringo*. He was too calm, too dispassionate. He asked the man's name and got a cold look accompanied by a moment of hesitancy before he replied, and even then he ignored the sergeant to address the lieutenant.

"I'm John Goethals." The man made a gesture. "This was my pack train."

"Yours," Mulvaney asked. "Or Lucky Lady's pack train?"

John Goethals gave Mulvaney another look of disapproval and addressed Lieutenant Leary. "I was hired by Mister Hamilton of Lucky Lady mine to take this pack outfit to a siding at the Gila. He gave me a map. Another two hours an' I'd have made it."

Mulvaney took two troopers to a dead mule and opened the pack.

Goethals growled and started forward. But Leary blocked his path, put out a hand and pushed. Goethals stopped.

Mulvaney arose, approached the lieutenant and handed him several ore-bearing rocks. Goethals said, "It was goin' by train to the smelter."

Leary handed back the rocks, considered the direction the raider had taken and said, "Best I can do, Mister Goethals, is leave some men here. It's up to you to find more pack animals an' get 'em down to the siding. Henry! Pick a squad and let's go after that son of a bitch."

John Goethals stood as before, leaning on his rifle watching. Pat Leary thought he had to be the most nerveless individual he had ever met.

Mulvaney would have added to that judgement but rode in silence. Sandy scoured ahead, the shod-horse tracks were easy to follow but the horse that had made them was no longer in sight. When Mulvaney came to ride stirrup the lieutenant said, "He can't keep it up. Henry. That mule's carrying a lot of weight."

The sun was well up, the dawn chill was being burned away but for an hour, or until the pursuers had to waste time avoiding vigorous stands of thornpin, it was comfortable riding.

A loping rider appeared in the distance heading straight for the soldiers. Mulvaney said, 'Sandy', and he was right.

Gomez was sweating when he reined to a halt and it wasn't that hot yet. There probably were other reasons but at the time no one was interested in them.

Gomez swung off the hard-breathing horse and loosened the latigo before facing Lieutenant Leary. "The mule give out. It's standin' in a patch of brush pretty close to bein' wind broke."

Mulvaney's impatience surfaced. "Never mind the mule, where's the rider?"

Gomez ignored the interruption. "His tracks go straight for a spell then swing north-westerly. He's favourin' his horse."

"And the *alforjas*?" Lieutenant Leary asked.

"The mule wasn't wearin' 'em."

The officer and the sergeant exchanged a look before the officer spoke again. "If he's carryin' them he'd better favour his horse. Lead off, Sandy, we can catch him now."

They rode for almost two hours, well past the drooping mule to country that had little brush, the tracks were plain enough for a blind man to follow. The country became rougher with fields of large boulders which had been there since the world cooled. Mulvaney rode ahead to prevent an ambush, but the tracks wove in and out among the huge old rocks without any sign of stopping.

Mulvaney waited until the others came up then stood beside his animal mopping his face because the heat had finally arrived. "That horse's got to have lungs bigger'n a bellows," he told the lieutenant and turned to scan the empty countryside ahead.

A trooper dryly said, "It ain't the lungs, Sergeant, it's the legs. One of them packs weigh over a hunnert pounds."

They continued tracking with Sandy Gomez out front. Their only halt was where the tracks led to a sump spring, the only speck of green in sight. They tanked up their animals exactly as the man they were pursuing had done, but he hadn't rested his horse and they favoured theirs; after all, whether they caught the bandit or not they would need horses for the return trip.

Sandy scouted until he broke clear of the boulder field where the tracks changed course again, this time heading more north than west.

Back on the trail Mulvaney said, "The son of a bitch can't keep this up, Lieutenant," and got a reply he might have expected. "Neither can we."

Sandy had found a tree and was standing in its shade when the others came up. He sank to one knee with a twig in his hand. "There's a pueblo west of here. Otherwise there's nothin' for fifty miles."

Pat Leary asked how far to the pueblo and Sandy tossed aside the twig and stood up as he answered. "Not far, three, four miles. It's one of them pueblos like the Acomas make. It's atop a mesa."

Leary dismounted, the others also did. He moved into the shade, studied Gomez's dust drawing, then looked in the direction of the pueblo. It was common knowledge Indians considered the Verde River Kid a hero. If he was at the pueblo atop a mesa the Indians would see his pursuers long before they got close.

Mulvaney offered a jarring thought. "He'd get a fresh horse sure as I'm standin' here."

Lieutenant Leary nodded, loosened the cinch of his horse, told the others to do the same, then sat down in shade. Mulvaney scowled but said nothing, which was just as well. What the lieutenant had in mind, and explained, was to wait until nightfall before riding to the pueblo.

No one objected, the men were tender-tailed and tired. The tree was a poor provider of shade for the men and horses, but they squeezed close, and while there was shade all that meant was that they were sheltered from direct sunlight, otherwise the heat was the same.

Mulvaney told the lieutenant their bandit would get a fresh horse and be over the horizon before sunrise, which was very likely, but in their present situation there was little they could do about that. Their animals had had hard use since leaving the Goethal battleground. As the lieutenant had mentioned, they were the same horses the men would have to ride back on, unless they were fond of walking.

Mulvaney made a hopeful remark, "Maybe the son of a bitch hid the *alforjas* at the pueblo."

"Maybe," Pat Leary replied, with scepticism. If the robber had got a fresh horse — or two horses and rode all night, his pursuers might just as well turn back.

A trooper asked how much raw gold the raider could have escaped with. No one had any idea but inevitably there was someone to make a guess. "Ten thousand dollars worth," the youngest among them said. No one argued, there was no point in doing so.

By the time dusk arrived all but two or three of the pursuers had already been sleeping for several hours. That was one necessity they would not be deprived of, but shortly before a sickly moon appeared the animals began fidgeting. They were not only hungry they were also thirsty.

It was this noise that got the men aroused and in the saddle again. It was supposed to cool off after sundown but not in the south-west. Someone had once said that in the south-west the earth absorbed and stored heat during the day and released it at night, which was likely. What they had not said was that rocks, boulders or even small stones stored heat and for a fact gave it off in the night. All a man had to do to verify this was place his hand palm-down on a rock hours after the sun had set.

But at least there was no cauldron-like big orange disk overhead as the men watched for lights and followed Gomez. They were almost to the age-old path leading up to the mesa before there was visible light, and even then it was so weak whatever its source, it could not illuminate a fair-sized room.

Sandy held up an arm. Everyone halted. Sandy swung down, handed Mulvaney his reins and started up the broad, dusty incline leading to the mesa above.

An old campaigner Mulvaney had selected to join in the pursuit spoke in a voice so quiet if it hadn't been a dead-still night no one could have heard him. "I been to pueblos before.

Sometimes, if there's trouble around, they'll have a guard at the top of the path. Otherwise they'll have dogs up there an' a pile of rocks."

Silence settled. They could make out where Sandy was hiking but because his clothing and the dark beige of the surrounding area blended so well the men had to watch for movement.

Above, where the trail reached flat ground someone cocked a gun. Sandy's shadow stopped and froze. Down below the lieutenant expelled a long silent breath. From up above a man spoke in a language none of the watchers below understood. Evidently Sandy had the same difficulty because he replied in English, and when that got no response he tried Spanish, and this time the invisible person with the rifle spoke in the same language. Sandy called to the men below. "He said no one's been here for months. He said we can't come up."

"Did you tell him it's the army?" Leary said.

Sandy turned back and again spoke in Spanish. This time the answer came after a pause and a deeper, more resonant voice spoke. "What does the army want here?" the second man asked in English.

Lieutenant Leary swung down, handed his reins to Mulvaney and started up the path. When he reached the place where Sandy had been immobilized a second gun was cocked. The lieutenant did not stop. He said, "I'm Lieutenant Leary from Fort Dix. If you fire the army will come back an' level your village."

He reached the top-out and halted. There was not a soul in sight, there were no longer any candles glowing. He could have been standing on a prehistoric mesa where an ancient pueblo had probably stood for six or eight hundred years without a soul in it, but that sensation passed abruptly when the man with the deep voice spoke again. "What do you want?"

"Talk," Leary replied.

An Indian appeared wearing a long

levita which reached to his knees but had arm holes instead of sleeves. He was old, dark with coarse features. He looked steadily at the soldier and said, "Talk, I listen."

Leary said, "A man came here. He is an outlaw. We want him."

Behind the expressionless old man someone hissed from the darkness. The old man said, "There is no one here. No outlaw."

Sandy came soundlessly to join the lieutenant. The old man flicked him a glance as Pat Leary spoke again. "But he was here. Did you give him a fresh horse?"

The spokesman answered with a bird-like nod of the head. "We gave a friend a horse."

"Did you know who he was? What his name is?"

Again someone hissed from the darkness. The old Indian did not answer immediately. Sandy tried in Spanish. "His name is what?"

The old man barely acknowledged

the scout's presence. He avoided a direct answer by saying, "The soldiers have no business here."

Mulvaney and several others came from the top-out to where the speakers were standing. This got the spokesman's attention and held it. Even in puny moonlight Mulvaney and his uniformed companions looked menacing.

The old man said," We have done nothing."

"You lied," Pat Leary said. "You said no strangers had been here. Then you said you gave someone a horse."

"No lie!" the spokesman retorted with spirit and the lieutenant cocked his head slightly when he said, "All right; then he wasn't a stranger. Mister, we're wasting time. How long ago did you give him a fresh horse an' what direction did he take when he rode away from here?"

Several soundless Indian men appeared like ghosts in the night-gloom. They were wrapped in blankets. They stood like posts staring at Sandy and the soldiers. Gomez nudged Mulvaney. Two of the broncos had suspicious bulges. Mulvaney spoke quietly to Pat Leary. "They're armed."

Leary continued to regard the old man. "One bad move an' the army will come here, dynamite your pueblo and kill your people."

One of the blanket-wrapped Indians, younger than most of them, said, "You come with me," and turned. Pat Leary threw the old man a look as he spoke to Mulvaney. "If I don't come back kill him first then the others."

The young bronco led Lieutenant Leary down a wide roadway between dark adobe houses which seemed to all be connected. Some had a second storey and ladders to get up there. Where the young Indian stopped there was a recessed wooden door set at least three feet into the wall. He leaned, pushed the door open and stepped back.

Leary smiled, fisted his handgun and gestured for the Indian to precede him, which the Indian did, and moved along a wall until he found candles and lighted them.

Leary got his first good look at the bronco. He was tall, his features were fine as he gestured. The *alforja* was in the middle of the room where someone had hastily dumped it. As Leary approached it the young Indian spoke English with no accent and none of the peculiar clipped, sometimes sing-song intonations of his race. He said, "He hid it here. The spokesman agreed to keep it until he could came back for it."

Leary sank to one knee, unbuckled the uppermost bag and reached in. As he withdrew a handful of small stones the Indian brought a candle. He and the lieutenant studied the stones in silence before Leary put them back into the bag and arose to say, "Why did you show me this?"

The youth answered candidly. "I was born here. My family has lived here for many generations. I am home for the summer. I am a senior at the University of Nebraska. Next year I'll enter internship. After that, two or three more years then I'll come back here and practise medicine."

Leary nodded. "All right, but why did you bring me here?"

"Because the spokeman would have defied you, and I know how the army reacts to something like this. He is old, most of the council are old men. My world and their world is different. They can probably live here safely for another few centuries — if they will recognize that they can't shut out the world."

"Did you see the man who left this pack outfit?"

"No. I was asleep when he came, but I heard the old men talking. I told them they had to give back the nuggets. I told them when they gave that robber a fresh horse they did wrong. I told them someone would be chasing him. I didn't know it would be the army."

"Do you know what the outlaw was called?"

"The Verde River Kid. My people think he is a hero. They laugh every time he isn't caught. They aren't the only ones."

"What is your name?"

"Bruce Singleton. That's the name of the family I live with near college."

Lieutenant Leary said, "Bruce, they'll kill you for doing this."

"No. My people don't kill. They will banish me. I will go back to Nebraska. Lieutenant, they did what they believed was right. Except for old ideas they are honest people."

Pat Leary stood gazing at the tall, sinewy younger man in a poorly lighted place full of silence. Eventually he said, "Which way did the Verde River Kid go when he left here?"

The reply was direct. "He rode southwest. There is a village called Wind Passes. They may hide him there. It is an Indian village but there is also a small town. It is called Bennington. Whites own all the stores and ranches farther out. He will never be found there if the natives can prevent it."

Leary went to the door, waited until the tall younger man had doused the candles then, as they walked in the direction of the waiting soldiers and Indians, Pat Leary said, "I wouldn't bet too much on their intentions after what you did."

Bruce Singleton's reply was revealing. "I won't. I'll leave tomorrow. But they won't do anything. The spokesman is my father."

7

Bennington

THEY left the pueblo riding in the direction the educated bronco had told Leary the Verde River Kid had taken on his fresh horse.

They rode without haste, their animals were tucked-up and lethargic. They had been watered at the pueblo but what they needed was food.

Mulvaney listened to the officer's story of the hidden *alforja* and asked a reasonable question. "What makes you think it'll still be there when we come back?"

Pat Leary looked at his sergeant. "It'll be there."

The night turned cold which was a harbinger that none of the riders heeded. They had eaten their last meal the evening before.

Sandy rode ahead to find the Indian village and its adjoining town. He found both but the sun was well above the horizon before he did, nor had his scouting sashay gone unnoticed, so when the other riders came up there were motionless Indians standing like sticks and in the town itself people were beginning to appear at the lower end where a stage road ran southward.

Sandy met them with a wide smile and gestured. "There's a stage company corralyard. They'll have feed."

Leary, conscious of the silent watchers gestured as he said, "Lead the way."

The town of Bennington had been founded by a New Mexico trader named Bennington, an easterner of some kind. He had been dead for six years when Lieutenant Leary led his unwashed companions to the corralyard in the middle of the settlement.

Two tall Indians met the strangers and called to the company-man who emerged from a lean-to office built against the palisaded north wall of the fortress-like large compound. He was short, bull-necked and usually had a cigar in his mouth. He did not smoke, he chewed. His name was Blevins. He had prominent gold teeth and a brusque manner. After the lieutenant explained who he was and why he was here, Blevins shifted the cigar from one side of his face to the other and said, "Yonder's In'ian-town, but mister, gettin' information from them tomahawks is like teachin' the blind to read. I'll care for your animals, it'll cost fifteen cents a day for corralin', feed an water. All right?"

Pat Leary nodded and was turning away when Blevins said, "Mister, the spokesman's name is Arturo."

Leary took his companions to the greasy-spoon to be fed and the proprietor, some kind of 'breed, dark, unshaven wearing a soiled apron, who hadn't seen men in uniforms for several years asked if the lieutenant's party was scouting for a larger force.

The lieutenant did not answer, the proprietor drifted away and did not return until his customers were out front heading for the Indian town, which was as different from the *gringo* town as night was from day. The Bennington section had fenced yards, trees, and *acequias* to carry water to every house. The Indian town had none of these things. It got water from a community dug-well, the houses were massively walled adobe and shade was provided by *ramadas* with brush on top to filter out sunlight.

The Indians were ready when the lieutenant led his companions toward the first house and asked for Arturo. The woman leaned and pointed. In Spanish she said, "He live there", pulled back and closed the door.

Mulvaney told Pat Leary the Indians were frightened which he thought was because they were hiding something, or someone.

Arturo was young for a spokesman, no more than perhaps thirty. His

English was accented but adequate. He was average height with a lean physique, sunk-set black eyes and shorter hair than was customary among tribesmen. When the lieutenant asked about a *gringo* in the village Arturo said there were always whiteskins in the village. This close to *gringo*-town it was to be expected.

Mulvaney took two men and walked among the houses. Arturo watched this before asking what the army wanted in this town.

Lieutenant Leary said, "I want the man who arrived here last night on a horse some pueblo In'ians gave him."

Arturo licked his lips, twisted to watch the sergeant and his companions, then faced Leary. "I was away last night. This morning I haven't been told of a stranger. You think he is here?"

Lieutenant Leary nodded. The spokesman at the pueblo had used identical tactics of delay and diversion. The officer looked steadily at Arturo. "Where is he?"

"Who?"

"The Verde River Kid. Mister, you lie to me an' when the army comes you'll have some weeping women. *Where is he!*"

Arturo's gaze flickered from Pat Leary to Sandy Gomez, to the people of Bennington who were watching and back to the lieutenant.

"He is not here."

"But he was here?"

Again the spokesman looked away, this time in the direction of the *gringo* town, and continued to gaze in that direction until Lieutenant Leary made a crooked smile and softly said, "All right. Thanks."

When Mulvaney returned to report that he had looked at all the horses and there was not one among them that was tucked up or showed dried sweat. Pat Leary nodded at Arturo and led his companions back to the white settlement, all the way to the corralyard where — the man with gold teeth was in earnest conversation with two other *gringos*. When the lieutenant and his companions appeared in the roadway entrance the palaver broke up, two of the palaverers walked past the strangers, nodded and kept on walking. The testy corralyard boss waited, cigar clamped in between his teeth.

Before Leary could speak Blevins removed his stogie, expectorated and said, "Who are you lookin' for?"

Leary gave a direct reply. "The Verde River Kid."

"Is that a fact? What makes you think he's in Bennington?"

"Tracks," Leary replied shortly. "Tracks all the way from a pueblo south-east of here."

"Well, mister, have you looked where tracks might lead around our town an' gone on?"

Leary shook his head. "No; we'll do that after we search."

Blevins chewed his cigar for a moment. His colour was high when he eventually spoke. "You don't have enough men to search our town, mister."

The lieutenant considered that a threat and was prepared for it. "If we got to — mister — we'll set down an' wait until the rest of the company gets here. An' if we find anything, I promise you you'll be the first one stood against a wall."

Blevins' face changed, the cigar stopped moving. He gave the lieutenant a look of pure defiance.

"Why would we hide anyone, tell me that?"

"I don't know, except that maybe — someone offered you a lot of gold nuggets."

"You figure we'd take the word of an outlaw?"

"For enough gold, yes, I think you would. Mister Blevins, you'n I are goin' to sit in your office. Just the pair of us. My men will search. If I hear one gunshot, if anyone interferes, I'll kill you."

"I don't carry a gun!"

"That won't matter, Mister Blevins. I'll fire twice and put a gun in your hand."

"That's gawddamned murder. I'll tell — "

"You won't tell anyone. You'll be dead. Mister Blevins, you can stay alive an' save me a lot of time — *where is he!*"

"That damned In'ian told you a lie. He ain't here."

Lieutenant Leary turned. "Sergeant . . . "

Mulvaney nodded and left only Sandy Gomez as he led off from the corralyard to begin the search. Lieutenant Leary took the barrel-built man with gold teeth by the arm, escorted him to the office, entered and gave Blevins a rough shove in the direction of a littered table and an old wired-together chair. "Sit," he said. Leary sat down on a wall-bench, lifted out his pistol and held it in his lap.

Blevins squawked. "Folks won't take kindly to soldiers searchin' their houses an' sheds."

Pat Leary's reply was given while the lieutenant looked the stager squarely in the face. "One gunshot," he said. "Relax, Mister Blevins. We'll just set here an' wait. Unless you want to talk."

"Sure as hell someone'll try to stop them searchers. Mister, this ain't one of your cities, folks who live out here use guns like city folks use handkerchiefs."

"I hope not, Mister Blevins. Just one gunshot, remember?"

Blevins sweated, the cigar moved jerkily from one side of his mouth to the other side. He leaned to open a drawer and the soldier raised and cocked his handgun. Blevins straightened up and did not move again.

Somewhere not too distant there was a loud argument between two men. When it ended the little office became as silent as a tomb until the lieutenant said, "I've never before seen a *gringo* town built up next to an In'ian village. You folks must get along, which is unusual, wouldn't you say, Mister Blevins?"

"Maybe. We gave 'em silver money

for the land where an old buffler hunter named Frank Bennington set up a trading post an' from there on the town just sort of grew. We get along with the In'ians. When Arturo told you we was hidin' someone — "

"He didn't tell me any such thing," Pat Leary exclaimed. "He wouldn't tell me anything. I expect that's how you folks'n the In'ians get along — you'll lie for them an' they'll lie for you."

Blevins's earlier defiance was watered down by time and personal anxiety. He still looked defiant but as he and the lieutenant talked his attitude gradually changed.

"Why are you after the Kid?" he asked.

"For raiding a mule train carryin' nuggets to be melted an' the gold extracted."

"By himself?" Blevins asked.

"By himself. He hit 'em in a barren stretch of country west of the Harquahala hills."

"Wasn't there no gun guards?"

Leary nodded. "There were four mules. He killed three and drove one off. Where it played out he took the pack and run in this direction."

Blevins finally leaned on his desk and clasped his hands. "So he got away with one of the packs full of rough nuggets."

Pat Leary saw the change in the other man's face. "He got away with it."

"How much do you reckon the load was worth?"

"I got no idea."

"Maybe six, eight thousand dollars' worth?"

Lieutenant Leary slowly inclined his head. "It could be that much. Mister Blevins, the *alforja* he got away with he left at the pueblo. The broncos gave him a fresh horse an' he rode in this direction."

Blevins leaned back slowly. "The loot is back at the pueblo?"

"Yes."

Blevins clamped down on his cigar.

"An' you seen it, know for a fact it's there?"

"Yes. Mister Blevins, my sergeant thinks the pueblo people will take it, hide it so's when we ride back we'll never find it. I hope they don't do that. If they do next time I come back I'll bring wheel-guns and level the place to the ground. But mainly, I want the Kid."

Blevins sat in thought for some time during which his cigar did not move. He squinted over the lieutenant's head at the roadway door.

Pat Leary sat on the bench, pistol in one hand in his lap, waiting. Not just for Mulvaney's return but for the gold-toothed man opposite him to make up his mind.

Their conversation and the other man's attitude and reaction left Pat Leary with a suspicion that whether Mulvaney turned up anything or not, the pursuit was not going any farther than Bennington. If the Kid wasn't hiding in Bennington or the Indian village, he was somewhere close by, and Blevins' questions had sounded as though the man who had asked them was concerned. Particularly the questions about the mule-pack full of nuggets.

An old man appeared in the corralyard. Lieutenant Leary heard him talking to a hostler. He picked up very little of the conversation but two words were distinct when the yardman said, "Not now."

Blevins listened too, and started to arise from the chair. Pat Leary raised the pistol and cocked it. Blevins sat back down and grumbled. "I got a business to run."

Leary said, "So have I. Just set easy, mister. The search hadn't ought to take much longer."

Nor did it. A few minutes later Mulvaney pushed into the office and ignored the cigar-chewer as he said, "He was here."

Leary looked up. "Was?"

"Well; maybe he still is but there's

a lot of sheds. He's got an injured ankle."

At that statement Blevins leaned forward. "Who told you that?" he growled.

Mulvaney faced the stocky man. "A bird," he growled back and continued to glare.

Blevins slowly leaned back off the desk, ignored the sergeant and addressed the lieutenant. "Liars come in dozens."

Mulvaney growled a response. "Yeah, an' so do folks who'd sell their souls to the Devil for a silver dollar."

Blevins' cigar was moving again. Pat Leary arose, leathered his sidearm and gave Sergeant Mulvaney a quiet order. "Strangle the son of a bitch, Henry."

Mulvaney moved around the desk, ham-sized hands curved. Blevins was a powerfully built man but Mulvaney was larger and even more powerful. Blevins dropped his stogie as he attempted to leave the chair. Mulvaney used one hand to slam him back down. His grip was vice-like. Blevins tried frantically to reach a desk drawer, Pat Leary anticipated the reason and as he drew his sidearm, raised and cocked it he said, "That'll do, Henry."

Mulvaney released his grip and stepped back, glaring but silent. Lieutenant Leary said, "Talk, Mister Blevins."

The stocky man considered the gun barrel less than fifteen feet away aimed at his chest. "I got nothin' to say, but by Gawd I'll write Washington about you!"

Pat Leary's gun hand was as steady as stone. "Mister Blevins, I got authority to shoot anyone who obstructs military law with violence."

"What violence!"

"You just now tried to attack Sergeant Mulvaney an' you tried to open a drawer to get a gun."

Blevins' eyes were wide, his expression showed fear. "All right, the Kid was here. That's all I know."

The lieutenant took two long steps and pushed the gun barrel within inches of the stager. "You lyin' bastard," he said, and seemed to move the bent finger inside the trigger guard.

Mulvaney rapped Blevins sharply on the side of the face with rock-hard knuckles.

Blevins jumped his stare to the door leading into the yard and back. He said, "There's a reward on the Kid. I've seen the dodgers."

Pat Leary straightened back. "Several rewards, Mister Blevins."

"How much in total?" the stager asked.

Pat Leary had no idea. "I don't know, but not as much as those mule packs he left back yonder. The difference is, Mister Blevins, you're seconds away from gettin' your head blown off, an' that's a fact. You'll never see those packs."

Blevins's shirt-front was sweat dark. He said, "Put up the damned gun," and when the lieutenant leathered his weapon for the second time the stager leaned forward again, but this time he did not clasp his hands, he let them lie atop the desk like dying birds. "You make damned sure I get them rewards."

Pat Leary promised nothing. "Where is he, Mister Blevins?"

The stager took time to put another stogie in his mouth and bite down on it before answering. "He's hid out."

Leary looked saturnine. "Is that a fact?"

Blevins ignored the sarcasm. "I can tell you where, but I ain't the only one's interested in them nuggets."

Who else is, Mister Blevins?"

"The storekeeper, the saloonman an' ol' Doc Phipps the pill pusher."

"How come, Mister Blevins?"

"The Kid come here in the night with a cracked ankle. Doc Phipps fixed it as best he could. Him'n me and the storekeeper talked to the Kid. He knew you was still after him. He told us if we'd hide him an' send you away he'd divide a pack load of gold nuggets he'd hid when you didn't give up chasin' him."

Mulvaney growled. Where is the son of a bitch?"

Blevins looked up at the Irishman. "You got to find him on your own. You understand? If the fellers in it with me figure I told you where he's at, they wouldn't like it one bit."

Lieutenant Leary returned to his bench and sat down. "Where is he?"

"North of town in an old abandoned In'ian pueblo that the In'ians ain't lived in for hunnerts of years. You can't miss seein' it. Go north and watch to the east, on your right side. But the Kid's armed to the gills. He told us he's never been chased as hard before an' if you don't give up he'll fort-up and fight you to the death."

Mulvaney moved away looking for something to sit on. Pat Leary considered the stager for a time in silence, then said, "I'm goin' to leave a man here to shoot you if anythin' goes wrong." Leary arose, jerked his head and walked out into the yard. He sent two soldiers to the office to guard the stager until

143

the command returned.

The soldiers entered the office as Blevins was rummaging in a drawer. One soldier growled, drew and cocked his six-gun. Blevins drew the hand back, watched the soldiers sit down, one on the bench Lieutenant Leary had vacated, and leaned back, rolled his eyes, and slumped.

One soldier, an old campaigner, asked if Blevins had a bottle. Blevins leaned to open a desk drawer. The old campaigner leaned across the desk and aimed his six-gun from a distance of no more than three feet.

Blevins put a bottle atop the desk, kicked the drawer closed and glared.

The soldier took the bottle back to his chair, handed it unopened to his companion and eyed Blevins with a dispassionate gaze. The other soldier took two swallows and put the stoppered bottle on the floor beside his chair. He smiled as he said, "Much obliged. Just relax, mister, we're likely to have to sit here a long time."

8

Close. Very Close

LIEUTENANT LEARY went among the yardmen asking about the horses. He thought they would be well cared for. What he really wanted was to establish a sound relationship, which he had no difficulty doing.

He asked about the countryside, the road, the traffic, the weather, the nearby Indian village, about some old Indian pueblo north of Bennington, even if the water-wells in the area had dried up recently, something which south desert residents had constantly in the back of their minds. When he was leaving the corralyard with Mulvaney riding beside him he did not go north, he went south, which Mulvaney scowled about in silence.

Not until much later with the sun sinking did the lieutenant lead off westerly for a couple of miles, eyeing the sun as he rode and finally, with dusk coming he made for the north country without using the road. Mulvaney finally understood part of what the lieutenant was doing. The part about spending the afternoon riding south then west he never did understand. Mulvaney was a direct individual. The part he did understand was that the lieutenant had decided in the afternoon to await dusk before heading for the abandoned old pueblo.

If the party had ridden northward in daylight anyone hiding in the mud ruins would be able to see them for a mile and more before they got close. Leary's idea was valid but he had overlooked one thing: he and his companions were not the only ones trying to reach the old ruins.

As was his custom Gomez ranged ahead, watchful and occasionally sashaying east and west. It was during one of these pauses that he heard a rider coming. People did not ordinarily lope their animals after night fall unless they had good reason and Sandy, for all his faults, had been scouting too long to assume what he heard was a traveller.

He studied the sound before positioning himself on the east side of the road for interception.

When the rider was visible he looked portly and a tad long in the tooth for night-riding. Sandy lifted out his six-gun, waited until the last minute, then rode into position to block the night-rider.

The man on the loping horse hauled to a stop and considered the grinning tame-ape of a human being sitting his horse with one hand pointing a cocked pistol from the lap.

Sandy asked the man his name and where he was going. Part of the reply was illuminating. That was the last part. The first part was a poorly concocted lie on the spur of the moment. The man said, "I like to ride after the heat is gone. It's my constitutional. Good for the legs, the back, the lungs."

"Your name?"

"Arnold Phipps. I'm a medicine man, a doctor."

Sandy nodded and gestured with the handgun. He herded the old man in the direction he knew would effect a meeting, and it did.

Lieutenant Leary drew rein as did his sergeant. Sandy repeated what the old man had told him and Mulvaney spat aside in disgust. Lieutenant Leary asked where Doctor Phipps was going and got pretty much the same story Sandy had been told, but this time Doctor Phipps added a few elaborations.

Pat Leary gestured. "You go ridin' for your health in the night carrying that little satchel that's tied to your saddle?"

The old man looked down and around as though surprised to find his medicine bag on the saddle.

The lieutenant had another question.

"How come you to be ridin' to the In'ian ruin? To warn the Kid the army's getting close?"

"Who?" Doctor Phipps asked, and while he could have been an excellent physician, even perhaps a seasoned surgeon, he never would have succeeded as an actor.

Leary said, "I asked you a question, Doctor Phipps."

"I carry the bag most places I go. In my line of work a man can encounter folks in need of care."

Mulvaney spat again. He glowered but did not say a word. But the lieutenant did. "Doctor, who told you to warn the Kid the army was coming for him?"

"Who told me what? Lieutenant, you're barkin' up the wrong tree. I told your man here, I go ridin' when it cools off. It's my way of relaxing."

Leary repeated the question. "Who told you to warn the Kid? Sergeant Mulvaney is real good at workin' folks over without leavin' a scratch. Sergeant

149

Mulvaney, help the doctor dismount."

Phipps grabbed the saddle horn in both hands and as Mulvaney walked toward him, he shrilly said, "There's a hurt feller. I was going to change his bandage an' see how he was doing otherwise. That's no crime is it? What's this country comin' to when — !"

"A sprained ankle, Doctor?"

"Well, you could call it that. It's more like a pulled tendon. Hurt it when he jumped off his horse an' stepped on a round rock. Them things is very painful."

Lieutenant Leary looked at the scout. "Any others headin' for the ruins?"

"Not that I heard, Lieutenant."

"Suppose you ride over there and sort of keep watch."

As Gomez moved toward his horse Doctor Phipps spoke again. "You're interfering, Lieutenant."

Leary agreed. "Sure am, mister. Now let's all of us ride together to your destination. Move out, Doctor. The sergeant'll ride with you. One bad move an' Mister Mulvaney'll use a knife. A gunshot would make too much noise."

Leary rode stirrup with the doctor on one side, Mulvaney did the same on the other side. The lieutenant offered the old man a cigar, which was refused so the lieutenant lighted it for himself.

As he trickled fragrant smoke he said, "Did you talk to Mister Blevins before you left?"

Phipps put a sardonic look at the officer. "Those two soldiers you left with him wouldn't let a child into the office."

"Then how did you know to warn the Kid?"

Doctor Phipps was an abominable liar, especially when caught unprepared. "I saw you fellers ride north."

"I'm sure you did but that don't answer my question, does it? How did you know where we were going?"

"I didn't know. I was just out taking my constitutional."

Leary leaned and poked the old man

hard in the chest with a rigid finger. "One more time, Doctor: how did you know, who told you we were headin' for the In'ian ruins?"

Phipps sighed. "Do you know Lester Dudley, the storekeeper?"

"No, just to recognize is all. What about him?"

"Les an' Gordon Mason from the saloon saw you leave town ridin' south. They was curious. They sent an In'ian to watch. When he told them you'd made a big sashay before headin' for the ruin — well, Lieutenant — they didn't have to be real smart to figure what you was up to, did they?"

It was a plausible explanation. Sandy might not have noticed someone trailing them. His interest was northward not southward.

Lieutenant Leary said, "Doctor, when we get close you'n I'll ride in alone. He'll hear two horses so you'll have to make up a story. Tell him it's Mister Blevins."

The old man'd had time for reflection.

The conclusion was elementary; a man in his seventies had no business getting involved in stolen nuggets. He sighed and said, "Too late, Lieutenant."

Leary was caught off guard. "For what?"

Doctor Phipps did not pursue the subject, instead he said, "Sure as I'm ridin' here someone up yonder's going to get shot."

The lieutenant agreed. "Most likely. I've heard the Kid's hell on wheels with guns."

Doctor Phipps rode several hundred yards before speaking again. "If you'll let me ride in alone, I'll dope him full of laudanum. He'll pass out then you can have him."

"Good idea," the lieutenant said. "Except for one thing — tonight you're not goin' anywhere alone."

Doctor Phipps covered another hundred yards before speaking again. "Gold makes fools of men, Lieutenant. Years back I was a surgeon in the Secesh army under Bobby Lee. The work was hard, the pay was good, except that a man's savings weren't worth the paper they were printed on along toward the end. That wasn't the only time I accumulated money only to lose it, and now this: at my age I wouldn't have lived to spend it anyway, but there I was, drooling like a child when the Verde River Kid offered the three of us his proposition."

Doctor Phipps drew forth a very large blue bandanna, lustily blew his nose and pocketed the big blue handkerchief as he said, " 'Hope springs eternal in the human breast', even when man's old enough to know the dream of strikin' it rich, one way or another, is so much foolishness."

Sandy returned to report seeing three pack mules and three saddle animals in a patched mud corral behind the old ruin.

For Lieutenant Leary this news was not only unexpected, it was also disturbing. Doctor Phipps said,

"Mex *arrieros*. They come up here, but anything usable that's cheap they take it down over the line and hike the price a hundred times."

Leary asked a question. "Do you know that travellers stop there overnight for a fact?"

The old man was squinting for a sighting of the ruins when he answered. "All I know is what I've heard. Personally, I've never left the road to look around those ruins. But according to what I've heard, yes, traders, wanderers, range men, even an occasional In'ian holes up there if they have to. It don't rain often in this country but when it does it comes down in buckets."

Pat Leary sent Sandy out again, but with orders not to get close enough for the men inside one of those ancient rooms with their massively thick mud walls to hear him.

Sandy grinned in silence and rode away. By the time he had reached the road he wasn't grinning he was asking himself why military men felt impelled to tell other men how to act and what to do as though they were the only critters capable of knowing the commonplace when in fact many men like the scout had been risking their necks most of their lives and knew more about avoiding detection and annihilation than most soldiers. Mulvaney was the possible exception, he and one or two old campaigners.

They were close enough to dimly make out the rain-washed adobe walls when Pat Leary held aloft his right hand. Mulvaney swung off and turned his horse sideways. He'd had three cups of coffee much earlier and coffee affected Mulvaney the way beer affected other men.

Doctor Phipps was slumped in the saddle. How much of that was the result of age and how much was due to his present predicament was anyone's guess. He spoke in a muted tone of voice when he said, "You'd have done better, Lieutenant, to wait until sunrise, surround the place and starve him out."

Pat Leary gazed at the old man. "How do you surround a settlement like that one with as few men as I've got?"

They dismounted, the lieutenant forbade smoking or talking. There was no sign of life or lights up ahead and because the mud corral was out back the animals Sandy had said were there could not be seen.

The *arrieros* complicated things; when Sandy returned leading his horse he wagged his head. "They have wine. Them Messicans travel good."

"Which part of the ruin are they in?" the officer asked.

Sandy shrugged. He had been unable to get close enough to see light, if there was any. "I don't know. Most of them walls got no windows. That's an ugly place."

Mulvaney said, "How many animals, Sandy?"

"Three mules an' three saddle horses."

Mulvaney swore in muffled disgust. "If the *arrieros* rode three horses an' led their mules that means they're inside with the Kid, an' that makes bad odds."

No one spoke for about ten seconds before the lieutenant jerked his head for Mulvaney to follow, told the others including Gomez to remain where they were and struck out.

There was a lopsided moon which gave off practically no light and hordes of stars which did no better. Otherwise the night was warm and men who had been in the darkness for any length of time could see fairly well but not for any distance.

Reaching the ruins was not difficult except that when they came up behind the corral the animals turned, ears pointing and stared in their direction.

They waited for someone to notice this. The men were inside and did not notice, at least there was no hint of movement.

Pat Leary went down the south side

of the corral, side-stepped where adobe deterioration had been corrected by spindly limbs of brush, some of which had been knocked free by rubbing or cribbing animals, avoided making noise and reached the south-west corner of the old corral where it was possible to make out one deeply recessed door with a curved top. He was looking for leaking candle light but this door, which opened inward, had been made oversized; when it was closed light could not seep through.

Mulvaney tapped the officer and gestured. Northward there was another door, actually a pair of doors wide enough when opened to allow a considerable mob to pass through. This, the lieutenant thought, would be the main entrance to a large room which, at one time many years ago, had been where residents 'made medicine', gave offerings to appease strange gods and implored them to send rain, less wind and no soldiers.

They retraced their steps and went

down the north side of the corral. Here, they picked up the scent of tobacco smoke.

Pat Leary crept to the corner of the corral, motioned for Mulvaney to stay behind and began a careful advance toward the double doors.

He was leaning, preparing to get closer when one of the mules brayed, a harsh, see-sawing sound that had none of the less harshness of a whinnying horse.

Mulvaney hissed. Lieutenant Leary went back to the corner of the corral. He and Mulvaney crouched against the rough textured wall.

A man emerged from the large room. Behind him, before he closed the door, light shone.

It was a Mexican *arriero*, one of those young ones who wore little bells down the outside of his leather trousers. The idea of the little bells was to attract women and had its origin in Mexico but could be counted on not to attract anything north of the border but stares.

He was smoking a *cigarillo*, each time he inhaled the tip glowed. He wore a low-slung holstered Colt. Without his enormous sombrero he looked like other rangemen except for the monstrous Chihuahua spurs.

He killed the smoke, went to the front of the corral and leaned there speaking Spanish to the animals. They came over where he was standing. He told them things in Spanish Lieutenant Leary would have given a month's pay to understand.

A second *arriero* came out. He was smaller, more fine-boned than the first man. He was also older but that would be hard to discern by weak skylight.

They conversed, smoked and leaned, in no hurry to go back inside. Pat Leary drew his side arm which prompted Mulvaney to do the same. Leary's idea was to wait until they were moving toward the double doors with their backs to him, then challenge them.

The Mexicans eventually turned back and at the same time another man came outside. This man was tall, leaner than the Mexicans. He spoke to the *arrieros* in faultless Spanish. One of them grinned, the other one laughed and said something back which Sandy would have understood, but Sandy was not there.

Mulvaney gently brushed the lieutenant's arm. "Watch."

"For what?"

"When he come past the door he was favouring."

Leary concentrated on the tall, lean man, who did not move until the *arrieros* reached him, then he hitched around favouring one leg.

Mulvaney came out of his crouch, pistol rising. Pat Leary jerked him down.

The three men opened the door, passed through and closed the door.

Leary looked at the sergeant who grudgingly nodded his head. They remained hidden until after the door had been closed then Pat Leary jerked his head and led off back the way they had come. Mulvaney followed but scowled at what he considered a retreat.

Leary went around where the hole in the mud wall had been patched with limbs and brush, leathered his six-gun and began removing the barrier. Mulvaney joined in, finally understanding what the lieutenant was doing; satisfied the Verde River Kid was inside, his idea was to set him afoot. As the mules followed the horses out of the opening Pat Leary watched with concern. He had isolated the outlaw but he had also done the same to the Mexicans. He'd had no choice.

He sent Mulvaney back to bring up the others, the prisoner too. While waiting he got close to the rear wall of the large room but if there was conversation in there he could not hear it through adobe walls somewhere between three and four feet thick.

He returned to the south wall of the empty corral to wait. Mulvaney appeared first, ghost-like and soundless.

He had Doctor Phipps with him. The old man sank down on the ground, clearly afraid.

Mulvaney had made a circuit of the old ruin with the doctor for company and it turned out that Doctor Phipps knew the ruin very well; odd for someone who professed no interest in it.

When Mulvaney pushed Phipps into a sitting position beside the lieutenant he paused briefly before speaking to throw a narrow-eyed look in the direction of the double doors. Then he said, "Doctor Phipps said there's a cellar under the place that some Spaniards made a hunnert years ago, an' some little rooms like jail cells only with no way to see in or see out."

Pat Leary looked at the physician, Phipps spoke dully. "The Spaniards locked In'ians in those little rooms for punishment." It was never pleasant being caught in a lie.

Pat Leary was interested in something more immediate. "Is there a way to get inside besides those doors?"

Doctor Phipps replied slowly, "There's an old caved-in dugout leading from the cellar out beyond. I'd guess if you scairt those fellers inside they'd run for the tunnel, except that unless those packers been here before an' explored the place they wouldn't know about the tunnel. I'm sure the Kid wouldn't know about it. I expect I'm about the only resident of Bennington who knows where it is. Of course the tomahawks in their village might know. They pass stories like that from father to son."

Mulvaney was annoyed by the old man's wandering conversation and very slow and deliberate, almost ponderous way of speaking. He told the lieutenant if there was no other way to get inside without being seen or heard they ought to try the tunnel.

Lieutenant Leary arose pulling the medical practitioner up with him. "Lead off," he growled.

9

A Bad Night

WHY the old-time Spanish conquerors would make a tunnel was subject to at least a dozen theories but speculations could come later.

They made a wide circuit to get around where Doctor Phipps began scuffing ground, pitched sticks and dead brush aside. He didn't find the hole, Mulvaney did. After watching the old man poking and scuffing, the sergeant went over much of the same ground. How he found the hole had more to do with the bizarre than with searching. Mulvaney scuffed in a slight depression and a small owl exploded almost in his face. Mulvaney recovered from startlement quickly. He had soldiered in the south-west long enough to have encountered ground owls before.

They were small creatures who lived and nested in abandoned coyote dens, empty snake pits, under boulders. Lieutenant Leary came over and kicked dirt until the hole appeared. He sank down and scooped dirt with both hands. Mulvaney was helping open the hole with Doctor Phipps mumbling to himself as he watched, when someone swore loudly around behind the adobe ruin. Leary looked up. "Someone discovered the animals are gone," he said, and stood up.

Whatever he might have done, such as rush to the corral to confront the Kid and the packers, was taken care of very abruptly when someone back there slammed a door and dropped a *tranca* from the inside.

Sandy Gomez, an unobtrusive observer through all this, ignored the others to dig. His entire interest was in the hole which under vigorous digging was beginning to assume a respectable size.

Doctor Phipps stood watching and mumbled something about the tunnel probably being caved-in. Sandy glared and dug harder. Mulvaney and the lieutenant helped, the mounds beside them grew as discarded soil was thrown aside.

Once, Pat Leary rocked back to assess the distance between the exposed exit at the tunnel and the nearest segment of the adobe structure. Mulvaney was digging and without looking up he said, "A hunnert an' fifty feet."

Doctor Phipps wrinkled his nose. He had caught the scent of musty, stale air. So had Mulvaney and Sandy. They both rocked back gauging the exposed mouth of the tunnel. Mulvaney said, "It's likely a lot larger an' Sandy can fit in there."

Gomez gave the sergeant a look of something close to horror. He had never gone into a tunnel but he had over the years heard stories of people exploring them and having the tunnels cave in on them.

Mulvaney saw Gomez's expression and wolfishly grinned. "It ain't big enough for me or I'd do it." Lieutenant Leary, taller than Sandy, but lean and sinewy bent to peer into the hole. It was like looking into the bottom of a well on a dark night. He groped with both arms, failed to find the walls or ceiling and pushed through the hole.

The soil was soft and damp but when he was fully in there it was possible for him to crouch without striking his head. The width was close to ten or twelve feet and while there were places where the earth had sloughed off he did not encounter a cave-in which would have blocked the tunnel.

He crawled back, poked his head out and addressed the sergeant.

"Go back by the corral. Sandy, you'n Doctor Phipps stay here. When I'm satisfied it's open all the way I'll crawl back an' you can go tell Mulvaney to start a ruckus so the Kid an' the packers will rush outside. I'll need time to find where the tunnel ends and get up inside. You understand?"

Gomez understood but was less than enthusiastic. "An' if they don't run outside? Remember, they know the animals is gone."

"If they find where the stock got out, Sandy, it could have happened from a critter rubbing."

"But they run back inside and barred the door."

Leary was tiring of this. "Do what I said, go tell Mulvaney to make a ruckus. No gunshots, just a lot of noise."

"Yes."

"No, not now, Sandy. Wait until I crawl back. You understand?"

"Yes, I understand."

After Leary disappeared back into the tunnel Gomez turned to the old medical practitioner. "Do I look like an imbecile? Why do they always act like I am?"

Doctor Phipps said nothing, the wise thing to do at the moment.

There was a chill to the night.

Somewhere northward a coyote sounded and even more northerly got an answer. Spring was past and summer was close, but there had always been dog-coyotes who hadn't found a mate when they should have.

Doctor Phipps hunkered peering into the hole. "Why would anyone make a tunnel?" he asked of no one in particular.

Gomez, assuming he was required to reply, said, "Them Spaniards was always digging. The In'ians said it was because they looked for caches of gold."

"But this is a tunnel, not a glory hole."

Sandy, with no reasonable answer, said nothing. He leaned to poke his head through the opening, heard nothing and pulled back. "Smells like a grave in there."

The old man nodded. "Naturally. Something like this would smell that way. Do you have a bottle? I'm getting chilled."

Gomez not only had no whiskey but would have traded a good, sound horse for a bottle and the increasing cold had nothing to do with it.

A shadowy figure emerged from one of the adobe doorways, this one with no door. He lighted a smoke and stood gazing at the sky, then at the surrounding countryside. Gomez and the doctor pressed flat without moving. Sandy wanted to reach for his holstered handgun but did not dare.

The smoker was wearing a sombrero that tilted in back, opposite to the way *norteamericano* stockmen wore hats.

It was difficult to make out much except the musical sound of large spur rowels rolling as the man walked.

The Mexican did an odd thing. After killing his smoke underfoot he crossed himself, kissed his thumb and turned to re-enter the doorless passageway.

Sandy whispered to the old man. "Gawd won't help him, not tonight."

Doctor Phipps groaned but said nothing. By now, except for being intercepted, he would have examined the Kid's ankle, rebandaged it if necessary and got back to Bennington and his bed.

When Sandy squinted at him Doctor Phipps said, "I haven't been a drinkin' man in almost eighteen years."

Sandy nodded sympathetically. "Maybe they'll have a bottle when we get 'em."

Doctor Phipps snorted. "Wine. Messicans aren't whiskey drinkers."

Lieutenant Leary poked his head out the hole, he was hatless and his hair had dirt in it. He said, "Go tell Mulvaney to attract their attention."

Instead of obeying Gomez had a question. "Did you find how to get up inside?"

Pat Leary looked at the doctor first, then looked at the scout. "Yes, I found the exit. Just go tell Mulvaney to attract their attention."

Lieutenant Leary pulled back for all the world like a turtle sucking back into its shell.

Sandy nudged the old man. "Let's go."

They went south of the ruin a fair distance before coming back on a course that would put them behind the mud corral.

When they got there, there was no sign of the sergeant. Doctor Phipps sank down with his back to the mud wall. Sandy said, "You stay here, I'll scout."

Doctor Phipps wearily watched the 'breed start around the corral toward the north. He closed his eyes; he was too old for this sort of thing. Someone's finger pressing into his neck brought the doctor wide awake. Mulvaney said, "Keep quiet."

"Your scout went lookin' — "

"I said be quiet," Mulvaney hissed, and crouched high enough to see along the north part of the corral. Whether he located Gomez or not he sank back down and spoke in a whisper.

"Did the lieutenant get through the tunnel?"

In the same hiss of sound Doctor Phipps related what had happened. The sergeant pressed a finger to his lips and tired as the old man was he considered Mulvaney's extreme caution to be an over-reaction. The men inside could not hear a normal conversation through adobe walls three feet thick.

Mulvaney drew his sidearm. Doctor Phipps was infected with some of the Irishman's anxiety and eventually he saw what had clearly made the sergeant so wary.

A man crossed the area a hundred or so feet from the corral moving from south to north. By feeble and watery light he could be seen to be carrying a Winchester saddle gun.

It was not Sandy Gomez, the stranger was tall, and it would not be the lieutenant, he was either in the tunnel or inside one of the rooms of the pueblo.

Phipps leaned. "Who is it?"

Mulvaney dug a hard elbow into the old man's side for silence.

Whoever was out there was moving not only cautiously but secretively. Once he halted to fade from sight in darkness. That was when Sandy came around the corner and joined Mulvaney and the doctor. Sandy leaned to speak and Mulvaney clamped a massive hand over the scout's mouth and used the other hand to point with.

Sandy did not see the apparition until it moved. When that occurred he leaned beside Phipps against the mud wall and watched.

Once he whispered. "Gettin' crowded out here."

Mulvaney raised a bony fist and glared. Gomez did not make another sound.

Out where there were burial mounds the stranger sank from sight, either squatting or kneeling. It was difficult to be sure but the sergeant thought the man was studying the back of the ruin, probably in the area of the doors.

Sandy leaned across Phipps to whisper to Mulvaney. "Lieutenant said for you to commence raisin' a ruckus."

Mulvaney was intently watching the burial mounds and did not acknowledge what the scout had said, but eventually he did, when the wraith reappeared northward but only briefly and moved beyond the vision of the watchers.

Mulvaney came up into a crouch, told Sandy to stay with the doctor, not to let the old man get away, and started a stalk of his own.

Doctor Phipps addressed Sandy, "He was supposed to raise a ruckus."

That omission bothered Gomez too. He raised up enough to see over the wall toward the rear of the ruin, also peered out where the sergeant had disappeared before sitting back down. Doctor Phipps asked if he had seen anything. Sandy shook his head. He was more worried now than at any other time since arriving at the old pueblo.

Doctor Phipps didn't help matters when he said, "The lieutenant'll be wondering why there's no distraction.

The longer he stands in there alone the bigger the chance one of them Messicans or the Kid will find him."

Sandy got up into a crouch, peered toward the pair of doors then turned his attention northward seeking some sign of Sergeant Mulvaney.

Below, the doctor did not let up. "If they find the lieutenant the odds'll be too big. They'll kill him because you can't make up your mind what to do."

Sandy sank down glaring. Doctor Phipps was not intimidated. He said, "His blood'll be on your hands an' I don't expect the army'll like it that you got one of their officers killed."

"Me!" hissed Gomez. "I'm a scout. That's all I'm supposed to do."

There was an abrupt sound of struggle close to the rear of the pueblo but northward. Doctor Phipps nodded his head without speaking.

Sandy stood straight up. The struggle ended as quickly as it had started. Phipps spoke softly. "Depends on who

178

got behind who, don't it?"

Sandy glared, leaned and pushed his six-gun against the old man's neck. "Shut up you old son of a bitch! *Shut up!*"

The cold was increasing which meant nightfall was drawing to a close. Gomez cocked his handgun, stood like a stone straining to hear sounds and came within a hair's width of firing at the whisper of leather over earth. Mulvaney stopped stone still. "Put that gun away," he said.

Sandy lowered it but held it at his side. Doctor Phipps looked up. "Sergeant, you look like you been culling wild cats."

Mulvaney ignored the old man, peered intently toward the recessed double doors and let go a long, shaky breath.

Sandy said, "Who was he?" and got a cryptic reply. "It don't matter. Throw some rocks against them doors." As he said this the sergeant groped for stones.

Neither of them were accurate stone-throwers but eventually they hit the doors. Nothing happened. Mulvaney told the scout to remain with the old man and went down the south side of the corral, past the place where the animals had got through and crouched at the south-west corner. The night was still, stars shone with the variety of brilliance that went with cold nights, and Mulvaney made a dash, flattened against the wall south of the double doors and let moments pass before using the butt of his service revolver to strike a door hard. He did that twice, then flattened again waiting for someone to look out.

No one did but something happened, an abrupt eruption of gunfire which was somewhat muted but easily distinguishable for what it was.

Mulvaney yelled for Gomez to join him. The old man no longer mattered. Sandy arrived in a cold sweat. Mulvaney told him to blow open the single door south of where they were standing.

Gomez turned, aimed and fired three times. The door was riddled but did not open for a simple reason, it was barred from inside by an oak *tranca* which rested on a pair of steel hangers, but it did accomplish something; from inside someone fired back twice.

Mulvaney used this distraction to empty his handgun against the double doors, one door in particular, aiming at its very old iron hinges.

The door sagged but the *tranca* prevented it from falling.

Mulvaney risked jumping around to kick the door, which sagged even more allowing candlelight to show past.

Inside, someone fired one shot, not toward the wrecked door, and was answered by another shot.

A man cried out in Spanish that he surrendered, that all this had nothing to do with him.

Sandy did not bother to interpret and it would not have mattered if he had, Sergeant Mulvaney was fighting; nothing like language would make the slightest impression or the slightest distraction.

For what seemed ages there were no more gunshots, no more outcries, just a great depth of silence. Mulvaney moved back along the wall to reload. Beside him Sandy did the same as he said, "Who was the feller you stalked?"

As before when this question had been asked, Mulvaney ignored it. There would be time for talk later. He had a recharged gun in his hand when he called out.

"You in there! Come out unarmed with hands over your heads or we'll storm inside an' kill everyone of you. You hear me?"

The answer came in a high-pitched, unsteady voice, this time in English. "I will come out. No shoot. *Quien sabe?*"

Mulvaney's answer was a growl. "Come out you sons of bitches!"

Again the man with an accent called back. "You don't shoot — please, *por favor*. I am coming out. Listen, *compañero*, I am only a trader. I haven't fired my gun in years."

"*Gowddammit, come out!*"

The man who stepped past the shattered door looked to his left, straight into the barrel of Mulvaney's gun. He saw Sandy and spoke in Spanish, running the words together.

Sandy responded by asking a question. "Where is your friend?"

"Dead. A man came out of the floor. I was unable to move because of that but Miguel tried to shoot. The *fantasma* dressed in a dirty uniform shot first."

Mulvaney interrupted. "Ask him where the third man is, the *gringo*, the Verde River Kid."

Gomez put it into Spanish and got a wide-eyed look from the *arriero*. "You mean the crippled man sent here by the Mother Church in Albuquerque to see if this ruin can be restored for a mission?"

Sandy's mouth fell open. Mulvaney

growled. "What did he say?"

Sandy related it exactly as the *arriero* had said it, then they stood staring at one another.

Lieutenant Leary stepped past the broken door, eyed the *arriero* and spoke in border Spanish, which was understandable to someone like the pack-train rider but otherwise and under different circumstances brought either bewilderment or laughter.

The Mexican did not laugh. He did not even smile. He looked at Pat Leary but clearly spoke for the benefit of Sandy Gomez. "The horses and mules made a break in the corral. He said he would find them and bring them back."

Doctor Phipps spoke from the rear of the corral where he was leaning. "No, no, my friends. He couldn't even find the horses and mules in the night, but a desperate man would be delighted to find other horses, already saddled."

Lieutenant Leary gestured toward the *arriero*, "Leave him. His partner tried to shoot me. He's inside dead. Let's go find our horses."

As the men with Pat Leary started briskly away old Doctor Phipps continued to lean on the mud wall softly smiling.

He eventually went over to the broken door, climbed through and knelt beside the face-down man with out-flung arms. The other packer said, "*Muerto?*"

Doctor Phipps looked up, nodding. He said, "I am sorry," in Spanish and climbed back outside.

The cold was less against the mud wall but there was no place to sit and his legs, which had troubled him lately, made even simple movement painfully uncomfortable.

He had been sitting on the ground out there for about an hour when the surviving Mexican walked out a ways, was not gone long and returned to cross himself and tell the medical man there was a dead *gringo* near the north-east corner of the pueblo.

The old man thanked the Mexican and continued to sit.

Dead people were no novelty to Doctor Phipps, even under circumstances such as the ones he had passed through since last evening. Let the soldier-officer go see who it was. Better yet, let the lieutenant take his sergeant with him.

10

Surprises

NO one asked the arriero how the Verde River Kid had managed to leave the pueblo. For the time being it did not matter. What did matter was finding him before he found their horses. Even afterward how he had escaped would be more a matter of curiosity than actual concern, but as far as the lieutenant and his sergeant were concerned, once the Kid knew of his peril it would not be impossible for him to slip out into the night. He could have done it when they were around in front digging for the tunnel opening. He could also have done it while his pursuers were hiding behind the west wall of the corral. There were too many ways a desperate outlaw could escape in darkness.

Only the doctor would have time to be philosophical, nor was he particularly upset that the Kid got away.

After the others hastened to the area where their mounts had been tethered Doctor Phipps walked through predawn cold toward the northeast corner of the pueblo and stopped stone-still where the light of false dawn faintly outlined a dead man lying face down with a Winchester saddle gun about ten feet away, evidently hurled there by impact when the sergeant had come up behind him.

It was Lester Dudley the Bennington storekeeper.

Old Phipps stood shaking his head. The storekeeper had become a victim of greed exactly as Doctor Phipps had been. He was also too old for this sort of thing. He was also too overweight and punky from lack of exercise.

The old man did not offer a prayer, he simply said, "Les, you was a damned fool. Well, wherever you are I expect you'll have better sense next time. Goodbye."

When he returned to the pueblo the Mexican packer had covered his dead companion with a soiled old canvas tarpaulin from one of the packs and was sitting on a chair smoking and gazing at the covered lump. He looked up when the old man came in, ground out the *cigarillo* and spoke in Spanish.

Doctor Phipps sat and also gazed at the dead man. He said, "It was unnecessary. He didn't have to go for his gun. It wasn't his fight. Are the others gone?"

"Gone," the Mexican said and went to work rolling another quirly. It was ten degrees warmer inside than it was outside.

The men hurrying through the night behind Lieutenant Leary paid no attention to the chill. They had other concerns such as hunger and weariness to plague them but as they hastened behind the officer they were only thinking about the horses. An old campaigner keeping pace beside the sergeant said, "Maybe he took your horse, Sarge."

Mulvaney was sucking air. He had never been and still was not comfortable moving fast on foot. He replied to the soldier between gasps.

"If he did, maybe you'n the others'll quit makin' fun of me for ridin' a horse that turns inside out when he's spurred."

Up ahead Sandy squawked. He had encountered two loose horses grazing along with reins that had been slashed about six inches from the bits.

It required time to catch the animals and by the time they had made squaw reins to replace the cut ones the sun was beginning to rise.

The old campaigner was working at making a suitable rein when the sergeant walked by. The old campaigner looked up sardonically. "Was the son of a bitch wearin' spurs?"

Mulvaney, still searching for his

horse, answered gruffly. "I don't know what the son of a bitch was wearin' but if I could get my hands around his neck . . . "

Lieutenant Leary was astride looking down when he said, "Get mounted. Sandy; scout for tracks."

Gomez nodded woodenly. What else would he have done! Someday . . . !

But the light was insufficient, at least for tracking from the saddle so Gomez walked and led his animal. There were many tracks. He was required to search out the freshest ones until one set of fresh ones headed south-east. There were no other tracks in that direction.

Mulvaney was riding double with a younger man, a recent recruit named Ben Whitley, who was large and heavy-boned. His mount weighed close to eleven hundred pounds. It was capable of carrying two men one in the saddle, one behind the cantle.

They could ride no faster than Sandy's progress reading sign like a bird dog, so when daylight arrived and

Gomez could work from the saddle they made better time.

It was Mulvaney who, with an excellent reason, had been intently watching the dawn-brightening world who held aloft his right arm.

Lieutenant Leary rode back. Mulvaney pointed, discernible now but which wouldn't have been an hour earlier, was a grazing horse which had not yet seen or heard the lieutenant's company.

When they veered in his direction the horse froze, head up, little ears pointing, and with both ends of a mouthful of long grass protruding from each side of its mouth.

Whitley asked Mulvaney if that was his horse and got back a growl, "How'n hell would I know? It's a damned good mile away."

It was closer to half a mile but dawn played tricks with distances.

The horse did not break partly because the approaching horsemen were riding at a walk, and partly because it was standing knee-high in a patch of grass, a rarity in this country.

As they got closer Mulvaney called to the lieutenant. "Stop here. I can usually walk up to him."

Everyone halted, Mulvaney swung to the ground and began a slow, casual hike in the direction of the horse. One rein had been stepped on and lost, the other rein was intact. As the animal watched Mulvaney it resumed grinding the mouthful of grass.

Mulvaney got a hand on the horse's neck, considered the broken rein and because the army's McClellen saddles did not have oil-tanned thongs from conchos he had to use his trouser belt, nothing a man would elect to do except under circumstances such as the one Mulvaney was in.

He rode back, halted, leaned forward and addressed the lieutenant. "A man with a popped ankle can't run."

They fanned out. The countryside had few trees. It was mostly grazing grassland. There were prehistoric rocks, some in jumbles, others separate and distant.

Sandy quartered for sign, found it and scouted warily. He was the eyes of the party, if something happened to him the others would persevere but not being seasoned sign-readers might never flush their man.

Mulvaney swung off and trailed Gomez on foot. The lieutenant remained a-horseback so the others did not dismount.

The new day steadily brightened. There was a hint of warmth to it which the manhunters would have appreciated more if they hadn't been as wary as quail. Somewhere in this rolling to flat cow country was a fugitive with an injured ankle. He could not have gone far in his condition so he had to be hiding, watching his pursuers. Whether he had a saddle-gun or not he would certainly have a belt-gun and because rumour had it that he was a dead shot none of the men hunting him did anything rash.

A particular jumble of big rocks seemed, in comparison with other places, to be the ideal spot for a hunted man on foot to hide.

But Sandy passed those fortress-like boulders to the east and did not raise an arm to bring the others to a halt until he was back a few yards from what seemed to be a wide, shallow and broad depression. Here, the tracks were less distinct than they had been back where Mulvaney's horse had been found, but Gomez had dogged them until he stopped, looking ahead toward the easterly rim of the arroyo.

Lieutenant Leary sent two men southward to find where the swale came up to reach flat land. He sent Mulvaney northward for the same purpose.

Pat Leary handed the reins of his horse to Sandy and walked toward the arroyo's rim. Behind him Gomez shook his head. No one in their right mind walked toward an arroyo where a desperate man with a gun could be hiding.

Leary halted a fair distance away, scanned the grassy verge for a hat, a head or a gun and saw nothing. The tracks were clear enough; someone had made tracks toward the arroyo, whether whoever it was had continued on out the far side was possible but there was no way to ascertain that without following the tracks down into the swale.

Lieutenant Leary cupped his hands and called loudly. "Come out! You can't escape."

Only an echo came back. Pat Leary was beginning to think no one was in the arroyo when a bedraggled, spindly-legged old Indian came over the lip of the arroyo. He wore a headband knotted on one side. He had no visible weapon except a tall staff which had been fire-hardened at one end.

Leary motioned the Indian toward him, turned and yelled for Sandy, faced the Indian and spoke in English very slowly, enunciating every word with care. The old man leaned on his staff, he appeared to have no teeth or very few, his bronzed face had wrinkles where most people didn't. Leary knew the type — blanket Indians, people who had nothing at all to do with anyone but their own tribesmen.

As they stood looking at one another Mulvaney came from the north, the other men came from the south.

The old tomahawk said, "You talk funny," in an accent-less voice. Leary reddened. He had made a strong effort to enunciate clearly with a lapse between words. He said, "What are you doing out here?"

"Hunting."

"Where is your horse?"

The old Indian raised his stick to point with. "Somewhere from here." He lowered the staff. "Crippled white man put his gun in my face. I said take the horse. He did."

Sandy, Mulvaney and the others looked stonily at the Indian. Sandy asked him in Navajo if he had known who the crippled man was and the old man answered in English. "No. I never seen him before, but he makes you listen when he pushes his gun in your face." The old man eyed Mulvaney's animal. "He told me I could have that one. He said it bucks like hell."

"How good is the horse he took from you?" Leary asked.

"Like me he is old, but he is tough and strong. You want to catch him? You can't do it standin' here talkin'. Maybe you don't catch him anyway."

Pat Leary went over to look down into the arroyo, returned, swung across leather and led the company on a fresh course, this one easier to follow because the sign was fresh.

Mulvaney rode with the old campaigner who said, "Henry, do you believe some things ain't supposed to happen? Look at us. Days an' nights, drivin' the son of a bitch from pillar to post without so much as layin' eyes on him. Henry, I think it's just not supposed to happen."

Mulvaney was scowling when he

replied, "It's supposed to happen. If we got to ride through the gates of hell, we're goin' to get him."

The old Indian was right, his old horse was strong. They did not catch a single sight of him and they travelled until early evening when they found a little spring and removed the saddles, bridles, buckled on hobbles and sat down in the heat of another dying day to rest.

The echo of distant gunshot aroused them. Within minutes they were astride and although their animals were tired they pushed them until they came in sight of a flat-roofed, massive-walled adobe building.

Behind it there were two pole corrals. When they got close enough to make out details it was obvious that an older grey horse had signs of drying sweat on him. He should have been head-hung and bone weary, but as the old bronco had said, his horse might be old but he was tough. The grey was standing with another horse, a bay with no signs of recent riding, peering intently in the direction of the fortress-like, ugly square house.

Sandy halted, slouched until the others came up and pointed out the grey with signs of hard use. Leary studied the horse. If their man was inside he probably was not alone. There was a maize and squash patch south of the house near the corrals. There was also a dug-well, enclosed waist high with adobe bricks. It had a cross beam from which was suspended a pulley, a wooden bucket, and signs of recent use; water still shone where the bucket had recently been lowered empty and hauled up full.

Mulvaney said, "Slits for windows."

Sandy finally spoke. He had made his assessment. "It's an old house, slits for fightin' off In'ians."

A soldier sounding exasperated asked why anyone would live in such a house in an area where there wasn't a tree worthy of the name, precious little feed of any kind and no shade.

Sandy had the answer. "The house was more'n likely abandoned. There's a water well an' if you take down a big breath you'll smell goats."

The soldier answered grumpily without taking a big breath. "I don't see no goats."

Sandy might have taken this up but the lieutenant, finished with his examination, said, "I'll ride on in."

Mulvaney spoke briefly and dryly. "If he's in there he'll shoot you out of the saddle."

Leary regarded the Irishman. "If he does you drag him out by the hair and shoot him from the knees up."

After the officer eased his horse ahead the old campaigner said, "Damned fool. The Kid'll get himself a hostage."

They dismounted, stood with their animals watching the lieutenant in silence.

Pat Leary rode around to the south side of the blockhouse, swung off where a massive cedar post had been tamped four feet in the ground, looped his reins in the steel ring and stood still, waiting. It was not a long wait. An old woman as shrivelled as a prune opened the door a crack and spoke in sing-song English. "What do you want?"

"I am Lieutenant Leary from Fort Dix. I'd like to come inside."

"You don't come inside whoever you are."

"Let me speak to your husband."

The old woman made a snorting, derisive laugh. "You're too late. He died six years ago."

Leary paused a moment before saying, "I want the man who rode that grey horse."

"You get him. He left the grey horse an' took my mare. I raised her from a filly. He rode away on her maybe two hours ago. I couldn't stop him, he had a cocked pistol."

Leary looked over where Sandy was studying the ground at the corrals. He called out. "Sign, Sandy?"

The scout shook his head and pointed toward the house.

The old woman slammed and barred the door. Pat Leary heard noises inside. It sounded like someone had pushed a table against the door. He rode back to the others where Sandy was waiting. Gomez said, "He's in there. Ain't no sign of a horse havin' left."

Mulvaney wiped sweat. Not having been near a razor lately he evinced a unique phenomenon, part of his beard was red, part was brown and part was iron grey. He squatted in horse-shade as he said, "After nightfall we can sneak in close an' get beneath them rifle slits."

Lieutenant Leary got back astride and returned to the house. This time no one opened the door. He spoke loudly enough for anyone inside to hear. He said, "Come out. Leave your guns inside."

There was no response. Mulvaney led his horse to the well to bring up some water for it. From where he stood he could see most of the east wall of the house. It appeared that the only window was in that wall. Not a glass window, but one where scraped rawhide of some kind, probably from a goat, had been nailed over the opening from the outside. It was not possible to see through such windows and it was just as impossible to see out, but the objective was never to use windows for visibility, it was to allow heat from the sun to reach inside and provide warmth in a territory where there were no trees and even mesquite was scarce.

Mulvaney led his horse where the lieutenant was standing, quietly told him about the window and suggested that if others would keep whoever was inside occupied watching the company on the north side, Mulvaney thought he could creep below the sill on the west side and knock a hole in the window covering.

Lieutenant Leary nodded. They both led their animals out where the others were waiting. Mulvaney went northward the short distance to the north-west corner of the house and was lost to sight in moments. No one asked questions and Pat Leary offered no explanation. He sent the men one at a time to the well to water the animals.

The old woman cracked the door and yelled at the last man to tank up his horse. "That water ain't free. By my count you owe me sixty cents."

The trooper led his horse close to the door, fished out silver coins and tossed them in the dirt near the door before leading his horse away.

The old woman hovered in her barely opened door. Sixty cents in silver was more money than she'd seen in a long time. She seemed to be prepared to go out and gather up the coins. Very abruptly she stepped back, the door was closed and the *tranca* was slammed into place.

Lieutenant Leary and the old campaigner exchanged a look. The soldier said, "I never seen anyone jump backwards like that, specially an old witch like her — unless someone from behind had her by the middle."

The sun moved, a few puny shadows crept into place, and somewhere in the distance bleating goats broke the silence. As the men watched an old man who relied heavily on a staff shuffled into view. He was watching about thirty goats and did not see the strangers until he was so close they made out details about him with ease.

Not only was he as old as dirt, he was also bent and warped, his shoes were tied with twine and one had been wrapped with croaker sacking. His trousers and shirt were patched, soiled and ragged. He had an old hawgleg six-gun shoved into the front of his britches but although he stopped stock still at the sight of the soldiers in filthy uniforms and a 'breed who did not look any more presentable, he made no move to draw the old gun, he instead allowed the goats to enter one of the corrals by themselves and leaned on his staff watching Mulvaney sneaking along the north wall.

11

The Verde River Kid

LIEUTENANT LEARY sent a soldier to bring the old man to him, which was done. The old man said his name was Obadiah Hemphill, that he and his sister had taken over the old adobe, had lived in it for nine years and ran a band of goats. He also said they'd had a dog but he had died three years earlier. The old man and the dog had taken the goats to graze every morning and brought them back every night. He said he'd shot seven coyotes so far this year.

He seemed guileless almost to the point of simplicity. He did not ask why the soldiers were here but the lieutenant told him anyway and the old man looked from Pat Leary to the house. He had, he said, left with the goats at about daybreak, then he faintly smiled. "If the feller you want is in there, mister, by the time my sister gets through with him he'll wish he never stopped here."

The lieutenant believed that, what worried him was that the old woman might try to use a gun, to which the old man wagged his head. "This here is the only gun we got except for a muzzle-loadin' shotgun and my sister don't know how to use it."

Obadiah faced the lieutenant. "I seen a man skulkin' along the back of the house."

Leary explained Mulvaney's mission. The old man stared at Leary over a long moment of silence before speaking again. "Suppose he shoots my sister? That kind of a surprise can get innercent folks killed. I've seen it happen, mister. Innercent womenfolk killed by accident."

Before the lieutenant could reply hell broke loose. Mulvaney had evidently reached the window. There were four gunshots, two sounded muffled and two were exceptionally loud, then there was silence until the old woman's screams made her stooped brother straighten up. Without a word he fisted his old pistol and scuttled in the direction of the house moving faster than Pat Leary would have thought him capable of moving.

He went out of sight around the south-west corner of the house, and the silence deepened. Pat Leary palmed his handgun and started after the old man.

There was one more gunshot, too loud to have come from inside the house. Leary halted at the corner of the house, hesitated then looked around.

The old man was kneeling where Sergeant Mulvaney lay on his back, he held his old pistol raised and was watching the shattered goat-hide window covering.

Leary did not go around the corner, as the old man had said, "'innercent' people got shot". The old man was clearly as tight wound as a spring. Any movement and he would shoot.

Pat spoke directly to him. "It's me, Lieutenant Leary," and stepped around the corner. The old man flicked him one quick glance then returned his attention to the window, his old gun poised and cocked.

Inside, the old woman's voice was quavery when she said, "Is that you, Obie?"

The old man answered. "It's me, Annie. Is he still alive?"

"I'll open the door, Obie."

"Is he still alive?"

"I don't know."

"Find out before you open the door."

For a long moment the silence returned and lingered before the old woman spoke again. "Yes, he's alive but he's settin' against the wall. I got his pistol."

"Is he hit, Annie?"

"I expect so, he's just settin' there."

"See if he's got another weapon,

maybe a derringer."

The old woman's retort was sharp. "I told you, Obie, he's propped against the wall like he's dead only he ain't because his eyes blink. I'll open the door."

Lieutenant Leary brushed the old man roughly aside, stepped in front of the door with his pistol cocked and ready.

When the door opened Leary kicked it wide open. It was murky-dark inside. One candle was atop a worn old table. The Verde River Kid was sitting with legs out against the west wall, both hands like dying birds in his lap. Visibility was too poor for the officer to see if there was blood as he stepped inside. The house had a sour odour. The old woman came from behind the door where she had been knocked against the wall when Pat Leary had kicked the door.

She stared at the soldier while massaging a skinny elbow. She said, "You didn't have to kick the door," and pointed. "There he is. Where's my brother?"

Obadiah appeared in the doorway, no longer stooped and holding his old hawgleg revolver in a firm grip. He brushed past the lieutenant and went to his sister. She turned on him like a catamount.

"I tol' you this mornin' I seen an omen in the sky but you took the goats out anyway. Now look!"

"Is your arm hurt?" the old man asked.

"When he kicked the door I was behind it. Yes, my elbow hurts. Obie, help 'em get that feller with the bad leg out of here. Tell 'em to go away."

Lieutenant Leary crossed the room with the candle in one hand, knelt and examined the soiled, unshaven man leaning against the wall who had heavy beard stubble and deep dark shadows under his eyes. Outside, men's voices intermingled where Gomez and the soldiers leaned over Mulvaney. One voice rose above the others as the old campaigner said, "If he's dead I'm goin' in there an' gut-shoot that son of a bitch!"

Mulvaney wasn't dead. He had a mean gash above the temple on the right side. He looked like he'd been butchering hogs, there was blood everywhere.

They worked over him, wrapped his wound and wondered how long it would be before he came around, if he ever did. His kind of wound as often as not cracked the skull.

Inside, the old man fumbled among some cracked dishes, wooden water buckets and unwashed bedding until he found what he was looking for; homemade *aquardiente*, not a substitute for whiskey, more nearly a substitute for embalming fluid. He and the lieutenant got three swallows down the Verde River Kid then the old man held the candle while the lieutenant searched for a wound — and found none. No injury and no blood.

He leaned back regarding the outlaw,

who was younger than the lieutenant but who looked older. Every sign of exhaustion was in his features. Even the pale eyes, when they came to Pat Leary's face, were lacklustre. The liquor worked fast. The Kid swung a slow gaze around, heard men outside talking and cursing, brought his gaze back to Lieutenant Leary and spoke softly.

"Who are you? You never let up, never slackened off. I rode down three horses an' still you come. I been chased by the army before but never by no one who kept comin', day'n night day'n night."

Leary asked if the Kid was wounded and got a negative and unsteady wag of the head. "My leg's killin' me. I ain't had anythin' to eat but cold tortillas. I been thirsty for a week. Mister, I just had to quit. I figured to get fed here'n sleep for twenty-four hours. Then I seen you comin', for chrissake, never lettin' up, always in sight down my back trail. Day'n night always back there. My leg was hurtin' bad when I come here. I figured to fort-up an' out-wait you." The Kid looked over where the old woman and her brother were whispering. "An' I ended up with a witch. That clanged woman even tried to steal my six-gun." The Kid again wagged his head before looking at Pat Leary.

"I never shot nobody except in self-defence. Mister, jail never looked good to me until today. Help me up."

Leary got the worn-down outlaw on his feet, told Sandy to watch him and went outside where Mulvaney was as limp as a rag with coagulating blood on his head, face and most of his shirt. The old campaigner looked solemnly at the lieutenant and said, "What a hell of a way to die. No flags wavin', no big battle, just lyin' in the dirt outside a ugly mud house shot by a son of a bitch not worth spittin' on."

No one disputed the statement, several men heard Sandy talking to the Kid and looked woodenly toward the doorway. Pat Leary had no difficulty reading their minds. Given half a chance they would kill the Verde River Kid.

Leary did not feel differently but he had reason to bring the Kid back to Fort Dix alive. The Kid's capture would be the only thing that would keep Major Erskine from giving his lieutenant a tongue-lashing for being gone so long, for having done things he was not authorized to do, and would arrive back at the post with gaunt horses and scarecrow riders.

The old woman came to the doorway, scowled at Mulvaney, went back inside and when she reappeared she had a small blue bottle in one claw-like hand.

She pushed through the long-faced men, knelt, told one soldier to hold Mulvaney's head and inserted two fingers into his mouth, held it open and poured liquid from the blue bottle, then she arose, backed away mumbling something no one understood.

Mulvaney opened his eyes, considered all the solemn faces and tried to get up. He got only into a sitting position and wouldn't have been able to do that if two men hadn't got down to brace him.

He looked at the lieutenant. "What in hell happened?"

"You got creased alongside the head."

"Did I kill the son of a bitch?"

Leary shook his head. "Someone fetch a blanket for under his head. Cover him too. Henry, you stay where you are."

The sergeant protested. "I don't hurt. Shaky is all."

"You stay there anyway," the officer said and went inside the house to face the old woman. "What was that in the blue bottle?"

"Laudanum. He'll feel like wrestlin' tigers until it wears off."

Leary looked at the old man who had his hawgleg revolver stuffed back in the front of his britches. The old man said, "I'd be obliged if you'd get that bastard out of our house."

Leary returned to the yard. It was getting dark. He said they would care for the animals, bed down and start back at sunrise.

The horses didn't fare well, feed was scarce. The men didn't fare too well either even though the old woman rasseled up a big pot of pinto beans with some fatback and molasses mixed in. They wouldn't have eaten any at all if they hadn't been hungry enough to chew the rear end of a skunk if someone would hold its head.

They had the Kid bed down among them. The old campaigner told him he was such a light sleeper he could hear a shadow.

The Kid probably did not appreciate the warning. He was as tucked-up from exhaustion as a gutted snow bird.

At the first streak of dawn the lieutenant roused everyone, even Mulvaney who looked and felt like he'd been dragged through a knothole.

His wound had stopped bleeding but his eyes watered and he groaned behind clenched teeth. He had the granddaddy of all headaches.

The old couple came out to watch the soldiers and their scout rig out and mount up. The old woman whispered something to her brother and he scowled at her. Fifteen minutes after Lieutenant Leary led his party away the old woman and the old man went inside to furiously rummage, retrieved six rocks which were at least eighty percent raw gold, more riches than either of them had ever seen before at one time. They had taken them from the Kid's saddle-bags during the night.

The trail back was taken slowly. Mulvaney had periods when he'd sag perilously close to falling from the saddle. A man rode on each side of him.

The Kid rode up with Pat Leary. He did not look any better in the morning than he had looked the night before. Once he said he could not believe it, soldiers usually made a sashay and went back to their post. He seemed a little in awe of Pat Leary.

They stopped once at a spring, the same place they'd recovered Mulvaney's horse, let the animals graze and drink, and the old bronco who had lost the grey horse came out of the underbrush. He looked steadily at the Kid as he said, "That's him. That's the thief who stole my horse." The Indian looked at Mulvaney. "What happened to him?"

A soldier answered curtly. "He got shot up alongside the head."

The old man dug in his parfleche, dug out some greyish powder and approached Mulvaney as he said, "This make it heal fast."

Mulvaney considered the Indian. "What is it?"

"It's spider webs mixed with special *teniente*. Take off the bandage."

Mulvaney made no move to touch his head. "If you got whiskey fine, but no damned stone-age medicine. Go away."

The old man leaned on his fire-hardened lance, fished into his bag and this time brought forth something that appeared to be a shrivelled, dried-hard pod with beans in it. He held it out, "Chew it."

Mulvaney looked at the pods in the wrinkled old hand and growled. "Go away."

The old man persevered. "Take it, chew it, in a little while you won't hurt nowhere."

"What is it?"

"Take it, chew it."

Mulvaney took the shrivelled, dried-hard brown pod, considered it as a soldier said, "Serge, In'ians got medicine we never hear of. Try it. You can't feel no worse."

Mulvaney chewed the pod with the Indian leaning and watching. The lieutenant told the old man where his grey horse was. The old man nodded but did not take his eyes off the sergeant.

Mulvaney gradually brightened. He

looked around and smiled. The old man walked in the direction of the corral holding his grey horse without a word. They watched him go in awe. Mulvaney stood up, slightly unsteady, but with an alert gaze. When the lieutenant thought they'd rested long enough he ordered everyone a horseback. Mulvaney still had an outrider on each side but he neither slumped nor groaned.

The Verde River Kid avoided eye contact and rode in brooding, demoralized silence. Occasionally he'd shoot a look at the lieutenant. When they had Bennington and the pueblo on its southerly outskirts in sight he eased up to ride stirrup with the lieutenant and leaned to speak in a whisper. "I got gold in my saddle-bags, if you're interested."

Leary was interested. He held out his hand. The Kid twisted to unbuckle the left pouch and rummage. He did the same with the right saddle-bag, straightened up looking wide-eyed at

Pat Leary. "It's gone," he said. "I had nuggets in the bags an' they're gone!"

Mulvaney laughed which startled everyone. His bandage was dark with dry bloodstain, one side of his head was badly swollen. He addressed the Kid. "You never had no gold. It's at the pueblo in packs."

"No! I took some of the richest stones. I had 'em in my saddle-bags yestiddy." The Kid's colour climbed, he twisted to glare at Mulvaney. "Somebody stole my nuggets!"

Mulvaney stopped smiling. "Are you accusin' us of bein' thieves?"

Pat Leary also twisted in the saddle. "Leave it be," he told Mulvaney. To the Kid he said, "You figured I'd let you go?"

The Kid said nothing, he rode erectly, looking neither right nor left. His neck and cheeks were red.

When they reached Bennington their reception was cool. The medical man had told them what had happened at the old ruin including their storekeeper getting killed. It was in the doctor's favour that he stated facts without embellishment, except to dryly state as a fact that as long as he lived he would never again become involved in a scheme to get rich if it was within the law or outside it.

They put up the animals with the dour liveryman with orders how they were to be taken care of, then trooped over to the café.

There, the coolness was particularly noticeable. Even the nosy caféman used only a minimum of words with them.

The prisoner was of considerable interest — and sympathy — but Pat Leary hadn't gone through discomfort and much else to lose his prisoner.

When they bedded down behind the livery barn, two men remained awake. Mulvaney was sick as a dog. Peyote buttons lasted quite a few hours but eventually their hallucinogenic sense of euphoria gradually diminished until it faded altogether.

Pat Leary hunted for the old medical

man, told him what had happened to the sergeant, told him Mulvaney needed strong pain killers.

The old man sold Leary a handful of small pills with instructions that they should only be given the sergeant one at a time on an empty stomach, and when the effect wore off the lieutenant was to give the next one to his sergeant. His last words were: "Don't get to feelin' sorry for him an' double the dose. If you do he'll go out of his head. By the way, that *arriero* tied his dead friend atop a pack mule and struck out for Mexico. It's a fair distance, Lieutenant. I'd bet the last half of it he'll be followed by *sopilotes*. Do you know what a *sopilote* is?"

"No."

"A buzzard. Would you like me to look at your sergeant?"

When the officer appeared with Doctor Phipps Mulvaney's eyes were watering again, he had mild tremors and had a half-empty canteen in his lap. He considered the old man blearily without speaking.

Pat Leary showed Mulvaney the pills, told him how he was to use them and Mulvaney considered the physician with the identical amount of warmth he would regard a sidewinder. "What I need," he said, "is another one of them brown pods with seeds inside 'em. Can you give me some of them, old man?"

Doctor Phipps shook his head. "The medical profession don't put store in tomahawk medicine. Brown pods, hard as wood an' you can feel seeds inside?"

The lieutenant answered since it was obvious Mulvaney was not going to. "Yes. That pretty well describes the pods. What are they? Mulvaney rode all the way here feelin' good."

Doctor Phipps's answer was given solemnly. "Those are *peyote* pods. In'ians chew 'em during ceremonial rituals an' dances. Half the time they don't feel pain, don't know their names. Do you have any more, Lieutenant?"

"The In'ian only gave Sergeant Mulvaney one."

"If a body chews *peyote* long enough they can't remember which tree their nest is in."

The old man started to turn away when Mulvaney said, "We got the son of a bitch!"

Phipps nodded. "So I've heard." Then he also said, "But you're still a long way from Fort Dix," and walked away.

They ate again at the café with Mulvaney responsible for the silence among the other diners. For that matter none of them looked any more presentable, except that only Mulvaney had a soiled rag round his head, a shirt-front stiff with dried blood, and watering eyes that had an unnatural glow in them.

12

The Last Fight

THE ride back to the pueblo atop its mesa was made without haste. In fact they rested more often than they had rested at any time on their way from Fort Dix. The men needed it. The horses needed it more.

When men complained of itching Sandy Gomez told them how the natives of this country bathed without water. They used sand. Ben Whitley asked if Gomez had ever tried it. Sandy answered truthfully.

"Just once. Maybe I didn't do it right, but for three days until I found water, my armpits was sore like they was on fire. There's invisible stuff in sand called micah. It got inside my hide. Even after I found a trough an' soaked in it the burnin' feelin' didn't slack off for another day or so."

No one mentioned bathing again.

The Kid now rarely spoke and rode like a sleepwalker. Evidently his physical exhaustion after being mercilessly tracked down was responsible for his complete demoralization. At times he did not even seem to hear when he was spoken to.

The old campaigner made an observation about this. He said, "For years he's laughed at posses an' the army, he's been a hero to the natives. Every time he got away with somethin' the In'ians an' Messicans felt like they had their own special hero. My guess is that his trouble ain't bein' rode down an' captured, it's that he can't no longer be a hero."

The Kid heard all this and rode stone-face into the lowering sun. When night camp was made, the horses had been cared for and the men sat around a little dry-wood fire, the Kid said, "Those old folks; sure as hell they stole my nuggets in the night."

The youngest among them, the recruit named Whitley had an answer to that. "I don't think it's possible to steal somethin' from a thief who stole it from someone else."

They struck out the following morning at sunrise and had the pueblo in sight on its tan-tawny mesa before sundown with Sandy far ahead. When they came close he signalled for a halt and rode back to tell the lieutenant he had a bad feeling because the purpose of building those pueblos atop high ground was so that anyone approaching could be seen long before they got close, and, as had been the case on their previous visit, there had been watchers up there. He said there was not a sign of a single person, not even where the trail went up from the ground below.

Mulvaney's little white pills kept him feeling a lot better than he looked. He squinted toward the mesa, spat and said, "Somethin's wrong," and the old campaigner responded in a way that was unanimous among the troopers.

"If they got In'ian trouble up there it's none of our business. Let's just go up there, get them packs and get the hell on our way."

Mulvaney glared at the speaker. "We ride up there like whatever's wrong ain't none of our business, an' do you believe whatever's goin' on they won't drag us into it?"

Ben Whitley said, "We can do like we done before, set down until it's dark."

The statement made Mulvaney swear at Whitley. "Whoever's up there, you idiot, has been watchin' us come up. They know who we are, the army — "

Stung by the sergeant's tone, Whitley interrupted to say, "Last time they was waitin' at the top of the trail. This time they ain't. I know they seen us. Let me ride up there alone. I'll find out what's goin' on."

Lieutenant Leary ended this argument by saying he would ride ahead and take Sandy with him. Gomez, who had been impressed by the total lack of life or sound from the pueblo, did not like the idea of riding up the path. He said, "Suppose it's renegade Apaches?"

Lieutenant Leary acted as though he had heard nothing. He jerked his head for Sandy to follow, told the others to remain where they were and started riding. As Gomez passed the old campaigner said, "It's been right nice knowin' you."

There was still plenty of daylight but because the sun was slanting away in the west, the butte on which the pueblo stood cast a wide, long shadow out where the soldiers were standing with their horses.

No one said a word as the lieutenant and the scout reached the beginning of the upward trail. If there was to be a fight, shooting the soldier and the scout as they rode up the broad trail to the top-out would be the ideal way to start it.

But there was no gunfire, in fact there were a couple of indications of life and neither was human, several dogs appeared to watch the riders coming up the trail. One dog began to bark furiously. The others promptly joined in.

Pat Leary and Sandy Gomez reached the plateau without incident and sat their horses in an eerie silence after the dogs slunk away in silence to disappear among the mud houses.

Leary said, "No candles. I don't understand this. The place seems to be deserted."

A phantom appeared from around a corner clearly poised for flight. Sandy called to him in Spanish. "Hey, man, what passes?"

The phantom did not leave his shielding corner. He seemed to the lieutenant to be very fearful. Leary spoke aside to Gomez.

"Ask where everyone is?"

Sandy put the question into Spanish and the phantom eased a little more into sight. With the sunlight behind him it was difficult to make out much except that he was thin with dark features. He finally spoke but in little more than a loud whisper. He did not reply in Spanish but in English.

"Did you see them?"

Sandy replied with a question. "See who?"

The phantom stood crouched like a coiled spring. "You didn't see them? They rode east."

"We came from the west," Sandy replied and Lieutenant Leary, who was tiring of this, addressed the phantom in English." *Where are the people?*"

"You want to see them? You are soldiers? Maybe you are with the others."

Pat Leary swung to the ground. "We're soldiers. We're not with anyone else. *Where are the people!*"

The phantom finally came fully into view as he raised an arm to point. "There. Some in the *deposito de granos.*" He moved the arm. "Some there."

Leary, who had followed the direction of the upraised arm looked at Gomez.

"What the hell is he talking about?"

Sandy scratched his head. "I think he said some people are in a granary. I don't know what else he pointed at." Sandy again addressed the Indian in Spanish. "Who put them in there?"

"*Mala hombres.*"

Sandy scowled. "I'll lead off," he said and with the wraith skipping from shadow to shadow he led his horse to the large mud structure the phantom pointed at with a rigid arm.

The *tranca* was on the outside, very unusual, most bars to lock doors were on the inside. There wasn't much reason to have a door-bar on the outside unless it was for the purpose of keeping someone inside. Maybe this was the pueblo jail but it was a very large room and when Lieutenant Leary lifted the *tranca*, because there were no windows although he heard the rustling of people moving he could see very little, and only near the open door.

Indians were sitting around the walls, silent, motionless, able to clearly see the soldier and his companion who could not see them very well.

The phantom entered behind the lieutenant and Gomez. In retrospect they would be considered a poor prospect for a warrior society.

Several Indian women left the large room. Emboldened, some men also left. One Indian spoke sharply to the phantom, who abruptly left. He then addressed the lieutenant. "They took the packs and put us in here."

Pat Leary said, "Who took them?"

"*Mejicano bandoleros.*"

"When?"

"Not long ago. We thought you were them coming back."

Pat Leary turned. "Get on your horse, Sandy."

He led off down the trail to flat country, hollered up his troopers and sent Gomez to read sign, no easy accomplishment on a nearly moonless night.

Tracking was difficult. The only shod-horse marks had been made earlier by the soldiers, all other sign was of barefoot animals.

Mulvaney looked like the wrath of God even in poor light but Doctor Phipps's little white pills seemed to work wonders. The sergeant rode between the command and the scout, hatless, grotesquely bandaged, filthy, and exasperated at the scout's slow progress.

They had travelled several miles when Sandy set up his horse awaiting the command. When it came up he shook his head. Shod horses scarred caliche, barefoot ones didn't. He raised an arm to gesture with when a rattle of gunfire erupted in the direction they had been riding. There were sporadic shots then another fierce exchange.

Lieutenant Leary took the lead with Gomez at his side. They did not push the horses. That gunfire had sounded to be no more than a mile or two ahead.

Mulvaney wondered what had caused it and no one speculated, they were interested in how close they were getting to the fight.

Close enough, evidently. A horse fled past them in a blind run, steel stirrups flapping, big-horned Mex saddle clearly visible.

To the lieutenant that meant the *bandoleros* from below the line who had found the packs at the pueblo and had headed south with them, had ridden into either an ambush or a deliberate armed confrontation, maybe both.

There was little time to speculate. The firing was bricking up again. Someone mentioned leaving the horses in order not to make targets. Lieutenant Leary ignored that.

Mulvaney, slightly ahead, had his horse shy so suddenly it almost lost its rider. A dead man wearing crossed bandoleers was lying face down. The lieutenant called Mulvaney back when there was another lull in the gunfire. Mulvaney came in reluctantly. Sporadic gunfire replaced the fusillade-firing and a man shouted in English. Mulvaney sounded flabbergasted when he said, "That was Lieutenant Bulow!"

Pat Leary was not convinced and slowed the advance to a slogging walk. Now, they could see occasional muzzle blasts and finally the lieutenant halted, dismounted and stood beside his horse. He gave no dismount order but every man behind him unloaded.

The man who had yelled in English before yelled again, this time an admonition not to leave cover.

Sandy rolled his eyes. Who in hell would expose himself in this kind of fight!

The lieutenant looked at Mulvaney, who seemed to be his old self and said, "Let's go a little closer." In a louder voice told the others to remain in place.

An odd thing about gunfire in the night — it always seemed closer than it is. Leary and the Irishman had sound to guide them but prudence suggested they should stop where there was a dead horse wearing a Mexican saddle.

Mulvaney said, "One dead one back yonder. One on foot. How many did them In'ians say there was?"

"Six."

Mulvaney snorted. "*Bandoleros* usually come by the dozen."

The gunfire ended, at least it was quiet enough for them to proceed slowly. They almost stepped on a Mexican belly-down peering westerly with his Winchester poised. He hadn't heard them, hadn't suspected anyone was behind him. He and someone opposite him about fifty or sixty yards distant had been duelling.

Pat Leary moved directly behind the Mexican as the man snugged his weapon back and lowered his face to fire. When the gun went off it was tilted skyward and its owner was flat out.

Leary jerked his head. He and Mulvaney separated a few yards. The firing had dwindled to an occasional shot. Mulvaney thought the border jumpers were leaving, and with good reason, whoever had faced them had never let up on the attack.

When the silence ran on two horses being ridden hard due south was the only sound. Mulvaney growled. "Two got away."

Pat Leary's reply was, "Saddle-backing, Henry. Somewhere around here are the *alforjas* they couldn't take with 'em."

A gruff voice called quietly in English, "Anyone hurt?"

He got back an irreverent reply. "Yeah, I can see two dead border jumpers an' an In'ian horse standin' like a statue with a pack."

The gruff-voiced man said, "Be real careful. See if you can get up to the horse. Slow an' careful."

Mulvaney leaned to whisper. "There was two packs."

Pat Leary nodded with little concern. He had recognized that gruff voice. It belonged to the pack-train boss from the Lucky Lady mine. He called to him, said who he was and got back a surprisingly warm reply.

"I never thought I'd see you again. By Gawd you couldn't have come at a better time. We heard 'em comin', didn't know who they was until they come straight at us with the packs."

Leary walked toward the gruff-voiced man who was not difficult to make out when he stood up. The packer shoved out a grimy hand and gripped hard. "Mister, I got to tell you, after soldierin' durin' the war I never had much use for the army, but so help me Hannah, I'll never say anythin' against the army again."

A solitary gunshot rang out. Everyone ducked and looked around. The *bandolero* Pat Leary had hit over the head had recovered and was running southward. One of the packers shot him in the back.

The pack-train boss told two men to look for the second pack animal and sent an arriero to catch the one standing like a statue. Those things done he led the lieutenant back where horse and mule harness was scattered, dug around until he found a bottle and handed it to the officer. Leary handed it back, sent Mulvaney to bring on the command and told the gruff man if he could catch the animals of the dead *bandoleros* he could pack them and head on south. To this the gruff man said, "Too late. The train we was supposed to meet came an' went."

"And . . . ?"

Leary had to wait until the packer had drunk from his bottle after which he said, "Go down to that siding, find a telegraph and send word to Lucky Lady what happened and am I supposed to wait down there for another train or come back to the mine."

The soldiers came up leading their animals, the gruff man eyed the animals and wagged his head. They had clearly been ridden too hard too long but he said nothing.

He had not lost a man in the fight, which was not unusual since the *bandoleros*, with no inkling they were riding into an ambush, and had reacted to be fired on in surprise with fusillades of wild gunfire.

One of the *arrieros* led in the Indian horse. Another man found the second pack animal where its lead-shank had become entangled in underbrush, otherwise there was a strong possibility it would have gone all the way back to the pueblo.

Time's passage rarely troubled fighting men. It did not occur to the lieutenant that the night was almost spent. He did not notice the predawn chill as he faced the Verde River Kid who had been surrounded by soldiers back where the command had been told to remain. The Kid said, "How many men did you lose?"

Leary answered curtly. "None."

"Who was them ambushers?"

"The fellers you robbed an' run off the pack animals."

The Kid considered the lieutenant in long silence, then tiredly wagged his head. "I'll remember you."

Pat Leary thought that might be a good idea. "Whatever-your-name-is — "

"William Smith."

"Mister Smith, unless I'm wrong as hell we got one more ride to make then we'll never meet again."

The command was moving south-easterly again by the time the sun showed above the horizon.

Mulvaney had taken a pill recently before riding stirrup with the lieutenant to say, "Damndest mess I ever imagined. Why did them border jumpers raid the pueblo? Lieutenant, I never heard of Messicans raiding a pueblo, did you?"

Pat Leary hadn't. "Henry, we most likely will never know whether they knew the packs were at the pueblo or just got lucky."

They reached Fort Dix two days later and, as Pat Leary had anticipated, a red-faced Major Erskine stormed across the parade where the bedraggled men on tucked-up horses came to a halt.

He walked down the line getting more angry by the minute. When the lieutenant dismounted and saluted the major halted directly in front and said, "Where in hell have you been! You know how long you been gone! Look at them horses!"

Lieutenant Leary spoke softly. "Major, that miserable lookin' son of a bitch on the piebald horse is the Verde River Kid. That's what you sent us out to do — find him an' capture him, an' it wasn't easy to do."

The bull-necked old officer glared at the prisoner. "That shrivelled, filthy, straggly-lookin' man is the Verde River Kid?"

"Yes, sir."

The major stood a long moment with hands clasped in back looking at the prisoner, then abruptly turned toward the lieutenant. "Well done! I figured you'd get him. I'll write up a recommendation, Lieutenant. Dismiss the men, have the animals taken care of and lock that worthless scamp in the stockade. Dismissed!"

Pat Leary handed his reins to Ben Whitley who, along with the others led their mounts toward the stable. Mulvaney personally punched and poked the Verde River Kid to the stockade and turned him over to a sergeant of the guard, a bullet-headed, cropped-haired man whose accent reeked of sauerkraut.

Pat Leary went out back to the washhouse, took an all-over bath, redressed in his second uniform with boots and socks, went back inside, dug out his bottle and turned to stretch out on the bunk when someone clearing his throat drew Leary's attention to the doorway. Sandy Gomez was standing there broadly smiling. Pat Leary pointed to a chair, handed the scout the bottle and, true to habit, Gomez swallowed three times, thanked the lieutenant in Spanish, pushed up out of the chair and went across the grinder in the direction of his hut built against the stockade's interior wall.

Lieutenant Leary stretched flat out on his bunk, swallowed twice from the bottle and was leaning to put it on the floor when Henry Mulvaney walked in wearing a clean bandage and a clean uniform.

Pat Leary gestured towards the chair and offered the bottle. Mulvaney declined, he had already drank with some with the enlisted men. He said, "Sawbones said the hair won't grow back where the bullet grazed me."

Lieutenant Leary looked at his boot toes when he replied. "Henry, you wouldn't never take a beauty prize anyway. You know why?"

"Why?"

"Because when you was born the doctor beat you in the face with his ugly stick. Go get some rest."

FIGHTING RAMROD
Charles N. Heckelmann

Most men would have cut their losses, but Frazer counted the bullets in his guns and said he'd soak the range in blood before he'd give up another inch of what was his.

LONE GUN
Eric Allen

Smoke Blackbird had been away too long. The Lequires had seized the Blackbird farm, forcing the Indians and settlers off, and no one seemed willing to fight! He had to fight alone.

THE THIRD RIDER
Barry Cord

Mel Rawlins wasn't going to let anything stand in his way. His father was murdered, his two brothers gone. Now Mel rode for vengeance.